DESIGN your Daring LIFE

WORKBOOK

Achieve Confidence, Success, and
the Courage to Have It All!

Connie M. Leach, Ed.D.

Design Your Daring Life
Copyright © 2021 by Connie M. Leach, Ed.D.

The scenarios in this book are based on real life experiences,
although names and details have been changed.

For inquiries, contact ConnieMLeach@gmail.com

Printed in the United States of America

Cover and Book Design: Carla Green, Clarity Designworks

ISBN paperback: 978-1-0879-5119-5
ISBN ebook: 978-1-0879-5208-6

College & Career Coaching Services | Design Your Daring Life
www.DesignYourDaringLife.com
www.ConnieMLeach.com

This book is dedicated to my granddaughters, Hayden and Addison;
my grandnieces, Carley, Charlotte, Claire, Hazel, and Edith; and to
every young woman who dares not only to be her amazing self, but to soar!

Contents

Special Thanks

It truly takes a village to write and publish a book. Much appreciation to my personal villagers: my writing coach, Jasmyne Boswell; my writing group members: Heather, Helen, Milda, Robin and Susan; my publisher, Carla Green; and my marketing consultant, Denise Cassino. Also, to my professional editor, Naomi Eagleson, along with Patti Hulet, for taking the time to proofread my work.

Thank you, to my sister Valerie, for our daily chats and encouragement.

Thank you, always, to my husband, George Leach, for your love and support in all of my countless endeavors.

A very special thanks to Reese K. Stame, for meeting with me every week to make sure the content and exercises would be of value for teens and young women.

Introduction

*"If you want to live a happy life,
tie it to a goal, not to people or things."*
—Albert Einstein, German Physicist

Dear Reader,

Design Your Daring Life is the book I wish I had when I was a teen and young adult, desperately needing a roadmap for life. Although many of the young women I see in my coaching practice today face different challenges than I did back then, they too, often feel confused and overwhelmed as they seek their best path forward.

As a college and career coach, I currently work with young women who struggle to figure out what they want for their future. They often feel stuck and discouraged not knowing how to move forward. Many of the strategies, activities, and stories you'll find in this book have come from my experience working with them along with many years as an educator.

Prior to my training as a coach, I was a teacher and administrator in public school education. Throughout my career, I have worked with young women in various capacities to help strengthen their confidence and leadership skills. In my research as a doctoral student, I examined the difficult issues facing teenage girls and what schools and communities could do to help. Later on, as a counseling intern I helped young women overcome emotional barriers that held them back from achieving their dreams.

My desire throughout my career has been to empower young women to make decisions in their own best interest and ultimate happiness. This workbook was designed for you to explore your possibilities in order to reach your greatest potential. My hope is that you discover something new and exciting about yourself thus creating your own best path to success.

The word *Daring* in the title is there to challenge and empower you to be adventurous and take the risks to go after what you want in life. It could mean having the courage to leave a job you dislike or getting that college degree you've been putting off. Or, it might mean finding someone special in your life, speaking out for a cause, or overcoming a physical or emotional challenge. Whatever daring means to you, the information in this book is meant to help guide you there.

The *Design Your Daring Life Workbook* offers techniques and exercises to help you understand the five main elements for achieving success. As you move through the book you will gain insight into what it means to be confident in your unique abilities and how self-doubt and fear can hold you back. You'll learn what it takes to build positive connections with others, explore the grandest vision for your life, and lastly, create your final plan based on your intentions for a meaningful and happy life.

Each section offers a quiz at the beginning and end to help you check your progress as you explore the content and complete the activities. A summary of the key points can be found at the end of each chapter along with a page where you can note the action-items you'll want to achieve.

Like, the quote above by Albert Einstein, it was discovering and persevering a well-defined goal that helped me create my own road to success. I've applied my years of experience and knowledge into the five Daring steps to help you discover what you're meant to do, and then create a plan to make it happen.

I invite you to gift yourself the time every day to read and do the activities in order to receive the best results. Being open to new ideas and having a willingness to take a few risks, can open up a world of limitless possibilities for you.

Please know that in spirit, I will be right along-side cheering you on throughout your journey in designing the most daring and joy-filled life...because the world needs you!

Yours in Happiness and Success,
Connie

P.S. The information in this workbook is quite comprehensive and may lend itself to working with a friend, colleague, or a professional coach.

Getting Started

In order to *Design Your Daring Life*, you'll need the following items as you move through the chapters:

- **Journal**: Find a special journal that motivates and inspires you to capture your ideas, thoughts, and experiences throughout the activities in this book.
- **Planner/Calendar**: There are many planners available in various sizes and styles. Choose the one that best fits your needs to handle all of your tasks, appointments and projects. The key is to stay organized and consistent by keeping everything in one place.
- **Folder/Binder**: You may want to organize information from the online activities in a folder on your computer or use a binder for printed copies.
- **Poster Board**: 18" X 24" poster board is ideal for the "Dream It" activity in Chapter One. A file folder can also be used.
- **Magazines**: Magazines – old and new – are needed for the "Dream It" activity.
- **Office Supplies**: Colorful pens, markers, paints, and pencils are optional, though it can be a fun way to draw, create, and imagine.

1

DARE TO
Dream Big

Imagine your grandest vision possible.

{ "Create the highest, grandest vision possible for your life, then let every step move you in that direction." }

— Oprah Winfrey, American Talk Show Host, Actress, Media Executive

Your Daring Life

What would a daring life look like to you? What are the possibilities? What could you do if there was nothing holding you back?

During most of my young life, I dreamed of becoming a teacher and having my own classroom full of young eager students. Because no one in my immediate family had ever gone to college, I was on my own to figure it out. For me, tackling college with little money and many obstacles, was the beginning of my own daring life.

In this section, you'll have a chance to imagine and explore what a daring life means for you. The word daring is meant to be subjective and based on your own unique wants and desires. It could mean traveling to exotic places, writing a series of books, starting your own business, being a leader in your community, or something else entirely.

Throughout this chapter you'll have the opportunity to expand your view of what life can offer. The exercises on the following pages are designed to help you explore those possibilities. When you discover what you want to pursue, your path will become clear. As Walt Disney famously said, "If you can dream it, you can do it." And, he certainly did just that! Here, on these pages, is a chance for you to dream big, too!

Take the quiz on the next page, to assess where you stand now in preparing for your future. Then retake the quiz at the end of the chapter to check your progress. Of course, this quiz can be retaken as many times as you wish.

Dare to Dream BIG
Pre-Quiz

What grandest vision do you have for your life? Take this quiz to see where you stand.

Directions: Read each statement below and put a √ in the column that best reflects how well that fits for you at this point in your life.

Dreaming BIG Strategies	Not Yet	Rarely	Often	I Got This!
I imagine a great future for myself.				
I know what I want for my life.				
I am open to new ideas and experiences.				
I know what I want for my work/career.				
I am aware of my passion(s).				
I envision grand possibilities for my future.				
I know what I want to achieve.				
I am aware of a variety of options available to me.				
I know where and how I want to live.				
I live a happy and enjoyable life.				
I believe I can create the life I want.				
I am creative and resourceful.				

The statements in the *Often* or *I Got This!* column are qualities you already possess. The statements marked in the *Not Yet* or *Rarely* columns are behaviors that you can develop and strengthen as you work through the activities. Retake the quiz at the end of the chapter to check your progress.

✎ EXERCISE 1.1: *What Does Daring Mean to You?*

What does the word "daring" mean for your life? Don't over think this, just write whatever comes to mind. Daring to me means…

_____

_____

_____

_____

_____

_____

What Possibilities Await?

In the following exercise you will create a "Dream It" board. This activity offers a powerful and creative way to explore possibilities. It is designed to bypass your thinking brain and connect directly to your inner and often subconscious passions.

Samantha, had recently been laid off from her job where she designed graphics in a small cubicle for a large tech company. She wasn't sure what to do next, though preferred something more fulfilling. Samantha needed to explore more options.

I encouraged Samantha to create a "Dream It" board where she would cover a large sized poster board with images and words that appealed to her, without judging her choices.

When completed, Samantha's board contained pictures of the ocean, beaches, along with the words: "tranquil," "breathe", "healthy," and "pleasures." She also included pictures of starfish, dolphins, and sandcastles. In the center of her collage were the words, "feel at home on the beach" and "whale watching."

> **"Sometimes I've believed as many as six impossible things before breakfast."**
>
> — Lewis Carroll, British Writer

While discussing Samantha's board, she realized how drawn she was to the ocean. It's not that she didn't know that about herself before, but this activity reinforced the notion of how important it was for her to live and work near the beach. She decided to volunteer at a local marine mammal center to find out if that might be a more satisfying career for her.

 EXERCISE 1.2: *"Dream It" Board*

This activity is designed to bring out what you love and what you want in life which are often overridden by what others expect of you. The "Dream It" board is an excellent tool that can be re-created many times over.

You will need the following supplies:
- 10-15 magazines
- 1 large poster board
- Glue
- Scissors

> The power in the "Dream It" Board activity is that it bypasses the judger in you, that says, "You can't do that," thus releasing your inner wisdom to be heard.

Directions:
1. Set aside at least one hour for this project.
2. Ask yourself a question, such as: *"What do I want for my future?" "What will make me happy?" "Where do I want to live?"*
3. Look through the magazines and cut out pictures and words that answer your question. Or, without asking a question, you can simply choose words and pictures that interest you. It is important not to question what you select. Simply trust the process and see what is revealed.
4. Trim and paste your items onto the poster board any way that seems right to you.

When you have completed your board, stand back and see what stands out. What do you notice?

> **EXAMPLE:** *I noticed I'm drawn to the design of various gardens. I'm especially attracted to the famous botanical gardens around the world.*

_____

_____

_____

What patterns or feelings were apparent?

> **EXAMPLE:** *My board is laid out in an organized and artistic fashion. It looks and feels well designed with bright colors and interesting shrubberies. It makes me want to draft beautiful yet environmentally friendly gardens for people.*

_____

_____

_____

What did you place in the center of your board? Is that something that is important or significant to you?

> **EXAMPLE:** *I placed a picture of a sporty yellow car in the center. I would like to take road trips throughout the country touring well-known public parks and gardens.*

A "Dream It' board is meant to be created often. It is especially helpful when you're feeling stuck by tapping into your subconscious intuitive desires.

_____

_____

_____

What did your "Dream It" board reveal to you? Did you discover something new? What action(s) will your take?

> **EXAMPLE:** *I noticed how important nature and gardens are to me. I have a desire to enhance communities with stunning landscape designs.*

_____

_____

_____

What feelings come up when you look at your board?

EXAMPLE: *I feel inspired to travel and explore natural landscapes. I feel energized by my passion for beautiful gardens that are environmentally friendly.*

> **"I am where I am because I believe in all possibilities."**
> — Whoopi Goldberg,
> American Actress

I feel _____

_____

_____

Use Your Senses

Another way to uncover your truest nature and inner passions is through your five senses and intuitive awareness. Petting an animal, smelling delightful aromas, hearing the sounds at a concert, observing the array of colorful flowers in a garden, or tasting the salt in the air near the ocean can expand your awareness of all that surrounds you. Playful and creative activities can help quiet your mind thus allowing your inner wisdom to reveal itself to ideas and opportunities as the "Dream It" board did.

Being near water can also have an enlightening effect. Answers, for example, come to me when I'm taking a shower or floating in a swimming pool. For others, simply listening to the sound of the ocean or sitting near a quiet pond can elicit solutions to their troubles.

 EXERCISE 1.3: *Tap into Your Senses*

Put pen to paper and list 10 things you could do to tap into your playful nature.

EXAMPLE: *I could...*

    – make a playlist of music/songs that motivate and inspire me

    – learn to cook with a variety of seasonings and spices

    – make time to paint with water colors

    – start a Pinterest page of my interests

    – explore nearby Botanical Gardens

1. _____

2. _____

3. _____

4. _____

5. _____

6. _____

7. _____

8. _____

9. _____

10. _____

*Which activity will you do this week?*_____

What Do You Wish to Achieve?

When you think about your future, what comes to mind? Do you imagine places you'd like to see, work you'd like to do, or special interests to pursue?

> *When John Goddard was a young teen, he sat down at his kitchen table and wrote three words at the top of a yellow pad, "My Life List." Under that heading he wrote 127 goals he would like to accomplish in his lifetime. Many of his goals were challenging activities such as exploring the Amazon River, climbing Mount Fuji, learning to fly a plane, and writing a book. He kept his list and checked off items as he completed them. Over several decades he had achieved most of his goals.*

> To learn more about John Goddard and see his famous list go to www.johngoddard.info.

Before you create your own Life List in Exercise 1.5, it is often beneficial to step back and look at what you've accomplished. Part of leading a fulfilling life is about not only learning and growing, but acknowledging and celebrating that which you have already carried out.

EXERCISE 1.4: *My Past Achievements and Accomplishments*

For this challenge, create a list of things you've already accomplished in your life. These can be big or small, such as learning to ride a bike, reading a classic novel, or winning an award. The point of this exercise is to help you acknowledge your previous achievements by writing them down.

Begin your list from as far back as you can remember to acknowledge the vast number of things you've already accomplished.

EXAMPLE: – *learned to read music.*

– *learned how to drive a car*

– *learned French*

– *learned to skateboard*

– *won a contest*

_____   _____

_____   _____

_____   _____

_____   _____

_____   _____

_____   _____

_____   _____

_____   _____

In the next exercise, you'll be creating your own life list, similar to what John Goddard did. Making a list of all the things you want to accomplish is another powerful way toward *Designing Your Daring Life.* You may want to post this list in a prominent place where you can add to it as ideas come to mind.

EXERCISE 1.5: *Create Your Life List*

For this challenge, create a list of things you'd like to experience or achieve in your lifetime. As you collect your ideas, you may want to think about places to see, things you'd like to learn, job/career choices, and hobbies and interests to pursue.

Looking through magazines, browsing Pinterest, or exploring other resources may help you generate interesting ideas. Start with 10-20 items and then add ideas as they come to mind. Remember to Dream BIG, beyond any perceived or current limitations!

EXAMPLE: – *hike the Grand Canyon.*

– *learn a foreign language.*

– *become a political leader.*

– *attend a major university.*

_____   _____

_____   _____

_____   _____

_____   _____

_____   _____

_____   _____

_____   _____

_____   _____

Look over your list and put a star by the items that you would most like to accomplish. Write your top two on the lines below.

_____   _____

Imagine Your Ideal/Daring Life

Many people go through life without thinking about or imagining what their life could be. They simply remain in their daily routines without putting much thought into what they could want or what possibilities are available to them.

Life coaches often use eight key areas of life to examine how their clients are currently living and how they hope to live in the future. These life areas often include the following:

- living environment
- education/personal growth
- work/career/money
- health/fitness/self-care/
- community/family/friends
- hobbies/leisure
- creativity/music/art
- spirituality/religion

> "Dream about your ideal life. Focus on it until you know exactly what it looks like. Then wake up and do at least one thing every day to make it a reality."
>
> — Source Unknown

In the exercise that follows, you will have an opportunity to imagine and envision what your most daring and ideal life might be.

 EXERCISE 1.6: *Your Ideal and Daring Life*

Directions: Look at the eight areas of life listed below. When thinking of these themes, what would be ideal for you? What would you want if nothing could hold you back? Write with as much detail and imagination as possible.

1. **Living Environment:** Where will you want to live in your most ideal life? Will you live near family and friends? Does the type of climate matter to you? How do you want to feel in this environment?

   EXAMPLE: I see myself living close to the mountains in Colorado because skiing is important to me. I love winter sports and want to find a job where I am close to the slopes. I feel energized when I'm in colder weather.

   _____

   _____

   _____

2. **Education/Personal Growth:** What will your ideal life look like in terms of furthering your education and personal growth? What would you like to learn? How do you want to feel?

   EXAMPLE: *I see myself having a post graduate degree in computer science and fluent in Spanish. I see myself staying politically involved keeping up with both the latest trends through magazines and online information. I want to feel informed.*

   _____

   _____

   _____

3. **Work/Career/Money:** What type of job or career do you want? What type of work environment do you prefer, such as outdoors or indoors? In what way(s) will your work contribute to society? In what way(s) does money fit into your future? How do you want to feel about your work/career/money?

   EXAMPLE: *I see myself as a millionaire able to afford travel, a large beautiful home, and an extensive wardrobe. I want to work in the field of medicine, eventually becoming a plastic surgeon helping those who have been physical disfigured. I want to feel as if I'm making a significant impact in the world.*

   _____

   _____

   _____

4. **Health/Fitness/Self-Care:** What will you do to keep yourself healthy and fit? How do you want to feel? In what way(s) will you provide for your emotional needs?

   EXAMPLE: *I see myself working out daily. I will be eating healthy meals, and meditating on a regular basis. I want to feel healthy and fit. Emotionally, I want to be able to care for myself by having time to chill and enjoy life. I'd like to be able to spend time at the beach.*

   _____

   _____

   _____

5. **Community/Family/Friends:** In your ideal life, what will family and friends look and feel like? What do you imagine your community will be like? Will you belong to a club or group?

   EXAMPLE: *I see myself living in a small beach town community. I will raise a family eventually, but not for a long while. I feel happy being around the people I enjoy.*

   _____

   _____

   _____

6. **Hobbies/Leisure:** In your ideal life, what will you do for fun and enjoyment? What are your interests outside of work? How will you feel?

   EXAMPLE: *I see myself hiking in the summer and skiing in the winter. Outdoor activities are very important to me. I feel energized when I have options.*

   _____

   _____

   _____

7. **Creativity/Music/Art:** In your ideal life, how important is having some type of creative endeavor? What might it look like? How might it feel?

   EXAMPLE: *I love to play the guitar and see myself playing in front of small groups. I can't imagine my future without music. I see myself enjoying a variety of live performances.*

   _____

   _____

   _____

8. **Spirituality/Religion:** In your ideal life, how important is spirituality and/or religion to you? What might that look like? How might you feel?

   EXAMPLE: *I see myself as a spiritual being, and I feel useful and connected when helping those in need.*

> "We all have possibilities we don't know about. We can do things we don't even dream we can do."
>
> — Dale Carnegie, American Writer

_____

_____

_____

Look over the ideas you wrote above. Circle the ones you want to pursue. What can you do now to get started?

- _____
- _____
- _____
- _____

{ "Let us make our future now,
and let us make
our dreams
tomorrow's reality." }

—Malala Yousafzai, Pakistani Activist

DARE TO
Dream Big

KEY POINTS TO REMEMBER

1. Use a "Dream It" board to discover your interests and passions.

2. Celebrate and honor your past and present achievements and accomplishments.

3. Imagine the highest possible future for yourself.

4. Keep an ongoing list of things you want to experience and accomplish in your lifetime.

5. Research places you would like to live and the type of work you would like to pursue.

6. Notice what you desire in each of the eight areas of life.

7. Explore your interests in fields of art, music, recreation, and other challenging endeavors.

8. Take the time to imagine and dream about a variety of possibilities for your life.

9. Seek beyond the day-to-day routines of daily living.

10. Believe you can create the life you want!

Dare to Dream BIG
Post-Quiz

After completing the exercises in this chapter, please take a few weeks or so to practice the concepts and then retake this quiz to check your progress. Also, the quiz can be taken at a later date to reassess your needs.

Directions: Read each statement below and put a √ in the column that best reflects how well that fits for you at this point in your life.

Dreaming BIG Strategies	Not Yet	Rarely	Often	I Got This!
I imagine a great future for myself.				
I know what I want for my life.				
I am open to new ideas and experiences.				
I know what I want for my work/career.				
I am aware of my passion(s).				
I envision grand possibilities for my future.				
I know what I want to achieve.				
I am aware of a variety of options available to me.				
I know where and how I want to live.				
I live a happy and enjoyable life.				
I believe I can create the life I want.				
I am creative and resourceful.				

How did you do? Did you experience any new discoveries? Did any of your checkmarks move into the next column? If you have any remaining √ in the Not Yet or Rarely columns, what action steps might you take to move forward in that area?

Dare to Take Action

1. After completing this section, did you gain some insight or realization about your life? What "Aha!" moments did you discover?

    - _____
    - _____
    - _____
    - _____

2. What goals or small action steps might you take to achieve your dreams? (It's helpful if you can be specific about what you will do and when you will do it.) Complete the following statement: *"I dare to create the highest vision possible for my life by...*

    EXAMPLE: — *researching a variety of jobs by Wednesday of this week.*

    — *starting a Pinterest page today to explore my interests.*

    - _____
    - _____
    - _____
    - _____

◆ ◆ ◆

"Dreaming after all, is a form of planning."
– Gloria Steinem, American Journalist

◆ ◆ ◆

2

DARE TO
Be Confident

Take pride in who you are and what you have to offer.

{ "Confidence is the only key.
I can't think of any better
representation of beauty
than someone who is unafraid
to be herself." }

—Emma Stone, American Actress

What Does it Mean to Be Confident?

Do you sometimes look at others around you and wonder how they can be so confident and self-assured? Perhaps you've noticed a friend or person at work who genuinely appears happy with who they are, rarely seeming to worry about what others think. Do you often wish you could be that self-confident and wonder what it would take to feel that way?

I can remember a time when I looked at others around me thinking they had their act together. I constantly played the comparison game always falling short and feeling diminished, thus allowing those thoughts to chip away at my own sense of self. It wasn't until I gained a better understanding of who I was and what I wanted in the world that I began to feel more capable and self-assured. Through practice and self-awareness, I learned that I could count on myself, to manage any disappointments and difficulties that arose. I began acknowledging my successes and felt worthy of the compliments and rewards that came my way...and so can you!

Building self-confidence requires knowing yourself: your strengths, interests, unique personality, and what you value in life. As you come to know your distinct gifts and abilities, you begin to better understand how best to navigate the world around you and are willing to take the risks necessary to achieve success. You learn how you as a one-of-a-kind person can take pride in who you are and what you have to offer. You learn to treat yourself with the respect and kindness just as you would a good friend. You then believe you are worthy of all that life has to offer.

> "The most beautiful thing you can wear is confidence."
> — Blake Lively, American Actress

The activities in this section are designed to help you gain self-awareness by better understanding who you are. Through the exercises on the following pages, you will discover what makes you stand out. You will take a deep dive into your personality characteristics and learn what relationships and career paths are most likely suited to you. At the end of this section, you will compile your findings onto a chart for an at-a-glance view of your best and most unique qualities.

The quiz on the following page is a great way to assess how confident you feel now. At the end of the chapter, you can retake the quiz to check your progress. Please note that this quiz can be retaken at any time.

Dare to Be Confident
Pre-Quiz

How self-confident do you feel?

Directions: Read each statement below and put a √ in the column that best reflects how well it fits for you at this point in your life.

Confidence Qualities	Not Yet	Rarely	Often	I Got This!
I treat myself as I would a best friend.				
I believe I am unique and deserving of happiness.				
I know my strengths and talents and am proud of them.				
I actively seek out things I'm most interested in.				
I am comfortable with who I am.				
I know what is important for my happiness and success.				
I use positive and encouraging language towards myself.				
I deserve all the good things that life has to offer.				
I am involved in hobbies and activities that interest me.				
I take care of my physical, mental, emotional, and spiritual needs.				
I honor my values and priorities.				
I practice self-care.				
I stand up for my needs, wants, and desires.				

The statements in the *Often* or *I Got This!* column are qualities you already possess. The statements marked in the *Not Yet or Rarely* columns are behaviors that you can develop and strengthen as you work through the activities. Retake the quiz at the end of the chapter to check your progress.

Are You Playing on Your Own Team?

Do you treat yourself with kindness like you would treat a good friend? Or, are you your toughest critic, putting yourself down when you don't meet your own or others' expectations? Being able to stay strong during the ups and downs of life, is essential in feeling and being confident.

When you demonstrate compassion for yourself, you are behaving in your own best interest. If, however, you treat yourself in an unkind manner, it is as if you're on an opposing team working against yourself. This self-denigration only increases self-doubt thus harmful to your overall health and well-being.

> "Treat yourself with love and respect, and you will attract people who show you love and respect."
>
> — Rhonda Byrne,
> Australian TV Writer
> The Secret

Some people believe that self-criticism works as a motivational tool. They say things to themselves like, "You're a total loser," or "You are a complete failure," to spur them on. While this tactic can work in the short term; overtime it can increase levels of anxiety and lead to lower risk-taking and ultimately failure.

In reality, long-term success and happiness comes from a positive belief in yourself and trusting that you can handle whatever comes your way. You and others are aware that you play on your own team, and will stand up for your needs, wants and desires.

Gina's roommate at college often ignored her. She would go out with friends, never inviting Gina to join in. Gina could have felt rejected, but instead she knew she could rely on herself to make her own plans. When her roommate would leave, Gina would call out to her to have a great time letting her know she was okay with each of them going their separate ways. Gina didn't wait for others to make her happy. She took charge of her own happiness and sought out clubs on campus that could satisfy her need for friends.

EXERCISE 2.1: *Write a Letter of Support*

Option 1: Find a picture of yourself when you were a young child. As you look at the picture, imagine telling your younger self about her future. What kind and encouraging words would you say to her? You might tell her about some of the situations she'll face when she is older and how she will be able to handle them.

EXAMPLE:

Dear Young Connie,

You have such a great future ahead of you. You are smart and talented and you can go after anything you want in life. Sometimes friends and life circumstances will disappoint you, but you will be able to handle them. If you stay true to yourself, you will thrive.

Dear _____,

_____

_____

_____

Option 2: Write an encouraging and supportive letter to yourself about a problem you are currently facing. Write it as if you were writing to a good friend.

EXAMPLE:

Dear Connie,

You got a low score on your exam today, but this one test does not define you. You love to learn and you are capable of doing well. Keep trying, don't give up, and you will do much better next time.

Dear _____,

_____

_____

_____

How Well Do You Take Care of Your Needs?

Are you sometimes busy taking care of other people's needs, totally unaware of your own? Perhaps you struggle, as I did, not knowing what basic needs were important to my own health and happiness. Once I learned these essential requirements, I was better equipped to not only care for myself, but care about myself.

When you make caring for yourself a priority, you shine. You convey to yourself and to others that you matter, and your confidence shows. Self-care is key not only to your survival, but also to your overall happiness and success.

> "It's not selfish to love yourself, take care of yourself, and to make your happiness a priority. It's necessary."
> — Mandy Hale, American Author

There are four areas that are important for self-care: physical, mental, emotional, and spiritual.

- **Physical**: Physical needs include eating healthy foods, drinking plenty of water every day, and paying attention to your personal and oral hygiene. It also includes getting adequate sleep, and exercise. Keeping yourself out of harm's way is part of your physical need for safety, including shelter and a safe school or work environment.

- **Mental**: Supporting your mental needs is about challenging your brain. This includes reading, note-taking, participating in discussions, working puzzles, or playing thought-provoking games. Good mental health also includes expressing creativity through music, dance, writing, art and so on.

- **Emotional**: Emotional support includes engaging in healthy activities that allow you to feel good about yourself, such as caring for a pet, connecting with a favorite friend or relative, or helping someone in need. Emotional support requires making your happiness a priority and surrounding yourself with people who care about your well-being.

- **Spiritual**: Your spiritual needs can be nurtured in various ways. This can include meditation, prayer, or spending time in nature such as walking on the beach, hiking through a forest, planting a garden, and so on. For some, being spiritual means participating in an organized religion. For others, it's the feeling of being connected to something beyond themselves, such as a bond with all living creatures or with the earth.

In what way(s) are you currently taking care of your needs? Which areas require more of your attention? How will caring for yourself improve your self-confidence?

 EXERCISE 2.2: *Practice Self-Care*

Make a list of healthy activities you can do to take care of your physical, mental, emotional, and spiritual needs. Do your best to fill in all of the blanks below:

Physical

EXAMPLE:

Go to bed by 10 pm on week nights.

_____

_____

_____

Mental

EXAMPLE:

Learn to play the guitar.

_____

_____

_____

Emotional

EXAMPLE:

Meet someone new this week.

_____

_____

_____

Spiritual

EXAMPLE:

Find a quiet space to work.

_____

_____

_____

Look over each of your responses. Choose at least one activity that you can begin right away!

I plan to _____ .

> **"When you recover or discover something that nourishes your soul and brings joy, care enough about yourself to make room for it in your life."**
>
> — Jean Shinoda Bolen, Psychiatrist

What Is Your Super Power?

You were born with unique talents and capabilities. I like to refer to these attributes as your Super Powers. People who are self-confident are aware of their powers and maximize them in their work and personal lives. The key is to know what your innate gifts are so that you can best benefit from them. In the next few exercises, you will be investigating your own Super Powers and how to best utilize them. The more you are clear on what you have to offer, the more self-confident you will feel. You will know who you are and position yourself in the best place to navigate the world around you.

In addition, your personal interests are part of your Super Powers. Exploring and cultivating a variety of interests such as astronomy, archery, filmmaking and so forth, is important to your overall well-being and positive sense of self. When you are doing what you love, your joy in life and confidence will show.

Erin, a first-year college student, struggled with her math courses. Her grades were lower than she had hoped and she felt like a complete failure. Dropping out of school seemed like her only option because she was so ashamed of her low scores. The problem was that Erin was focusing on her perceived negative qualities instead of paying attention to what she did well. She had let that one subject ruin her entire undergrad experience.

> **"The ultimate dream in life is to be able to do what you love and learn something from it."**
> — Jennifer Love Hewitt, American Actress

In our coaching session, I challenged Erin to a little game. I asked her to list 10 things she believed she was good at and/or things that interested her. I challenged her to take her journal with her wherever she went and to write down her observations. My intent was to redirect her focus from her perceived failings to her successes.

At first, Erin struggled with this task. She simply could not think of one positive quality about herself. I helped her get started by pointing out that she was always prepared for our meetings. Erin agreed and wrote "organized" on her list. Being organized was a Super Power of Erin's, one that she had overlooked.

The plan was, for her to write down any compliments she might receive and things that interested her. For example, if someone noticed her artwork, she would write down "good at drawing." She might also write art as an interest. Nothing was too big or too small to go on her list.

At our next meeting Erin couldn't wait to show me her list of 20+ items including: "good at math," "like to meet new people," "good at helping my brother," "neat handwriting," "interested in playing and watching tennis." She had begun to recognize the compliments, skills, and interests she had failed to notice before. By acknowledging her good qualities, Erin's self-confidence grew as well as her grades.

> According to positive psychology, people who honor their core strengths and interests tend to live happier lives.

In the following activity, you will create a list of your own Super Powers, which include your talents (things you're inherently good at) and things you enjoy doing. You may want to think about the things in which you excel, like sports or computers. Those skills and pastime pursuits can often lead to a future career. For example, an attraction to clothing may lead to a job in costume design or a love of sea animals can lead to becoming a Marine Mammal Trainer or an Aquatic Veterinarian. In other words, your interests and talents matter.

Many young women tend to focus on what is wrong with them rather than what is fantastic about themselves. This simple, yet powerful exercise, is designed to re-train your brain to focus on your positive attributes and interests in order to build confidence. Your Super Powers illustrate how you shine in the world, the very characteristics that make you unique.

 EXERCISE 2.3: *List Your Super Powers*

As you go about your day-to-day activities, notice your Super Powers which include your talents (things you're inherently good at) and interests (things you enjoy) and write them down on the lines below. Aim for 10 or 20 to get started.

EXAMPLE:

- *I'm good with numbers*   – *I learn quickly*

- *I enjoy horror movies*   – *I'm great at building things*

- *I love working with animals*   – *I am drawn to all types of music*

_____   _____

_____   _____

_____   _____

_____   _____

_____   _____

_____   _____

_____   _____

_____   _____

_____   _____

_____   _____

Next, challenge yourself to grow your list to 50 or 100!

What are your top Super Powers?

_____   _____

_____   _____

_____   _____

After completing this exercise, what did you notice about yourself?

_____

_____

_____

What Are Your Unique Personality Characteristics?

Learning about your personality can help you have a deeper knowledge of who you are and how you best interact with others. Your confidence builds when you understand and acknowledge why you do the things the way you do. People who are self-assured know their strengths and how their unique abilities can best be applied in life.

I often refer my coaching clients to some of the online personality assessments available on the Internet as a fun way to explore their unique characteristics. This information can give you insight into possible attributes you may have undervalued and, therefore, expand additional career possibilities.

While much of the findings can reveal quite a bit about you, it is up to you to determine what sounds true for you and what does not. What I've found from working with clients, is that the strength in these assessments does not come from the specific results per se, but from the insights they can discover about themselves. If, for example, the report indicates they would make a great salesperson and they don't agree, that realization presents helpful feedback. On the other hand, a small nugget of information can motivate a client toward a new direction, a new possibility, and renewed motivation. For example, if a report shows that you are a big picture thinker and are miserable managing day-to-day tasks, and that sounds true for you, then the information may be helpful in making an advantageous career choice. The power comes in thoughtfully considering the information each of these assessments offer.

Below are a few of the online personality tests I like to use with my clients:

- **16personalities.com**: This quiz is one of my favorites because it offers a free report with basic information about your personality. It is fun to take and easy to understand. You'll receive a four-letter personality character, such as Defender (ISFJ). A fifth letter is given to represent how you tend to handle life's challenges, with (A) Assertive and (T) Turbulent. A premiere report is offered for a fee if you would like to receive a more detailed printout.

- **Personalityclub.com**: This website offers a quick, free, and simple way to identify your four-letter personality type. In addition, attractive printouts for each personality are available along with short descriptions.

- **MBTIonline.com**: The popular Myers Briggs Type Indicator, offers a four-letter detailed personality report. This quiz is a bit pricey but includes personalized information in areas of relationships, well-being, and personal development along with lifetime access.

- **Keirsey.com**: The Keirsey Temperament Sorter provides a very detailed report in several categories including careers, leadership, relationships, and selling/buying. Each report has a fairly hefty fee, although the information they present is quite extensive and useful.

- **Standout.tmbc.com**: This assessment, by Marcus Buckingham, an expert on strengths, reveals your top two roles and then combines them to represent your unique way of making a difference in the world. At the time of printing this book, the charge for the online assessment was $15.00. The results provide insight into your greatest value in the workplace. The language provided in this detailed and extensive report, can be quite useful especially if you are currently seeking employment.

 EXERCISE 2.4: *Uncover Your Personality Type*

Choose one or more of the personality quizzes previously listed. Read through the report to discover your strengths and characteristics. You may want to print out your results and place them in a notebook, binder, or save to your computer, which can later be used in a job interview, resumé, school application, and so on.

What key points did the assessment(s) reveal about you?

- _____
- _____
- _____
- _____
- _____

Did you discover any possible career ideas?

- _____
- _____

- _____
- _____
- _____

What might you do with his information? What actions might you take?

- _____
- _____
- _____
- _____
- _____

Expand Your Personality

As human beings we each have the ability to use all personality traits, though we often limit ourselves. The traits that make us feel good are our strongest traits which we tend to use most often. They are usually the qualities for which we have been praised.

Nadia was a college student who always made straight A's. She spent most of her time studying and had little time to have fun and hang out with friends. Her parents and teachers always acknowledged and celebrated her accomplishments. Though Nadia was happy with her success, she sometimes felt she was missing out. I introduced Nadia to the Personality Trait list and asked her to choose the ones that were her strongest qualities. She immediately chose intellectual, organized, persistent, and serious.

Nadia had selected the traits that friends and family would readily recognize in her. While those were great attributes to have, Nadia, was limiting herself by not accessing a variety of other traits, and I urged her to choose some traits she would like to have, yet rarely used.

Nadia looked over the list again looking for traits she would like to use more often. She selected outgoing, fun-loving, and adventurous. Those were traits she tended to shy away from. From this list, Nadia chose adventurous as the one she would focus on for the following week. Together, we brainstormed a list of possible actions she could take to be more adventurous, some of which included joining a hiking group, meeting new people, and working on a community service project. Nadia decided to volunteer at a local food bank; something she had thought of doing before but never took the risk. Focusing on her seldom used trait helped her strengthen and trust it more often.

In the next exercise you, too, will have a chance to boost your personality as Nadia did. You'll identify the traits that are strongest for you and the traits you would like to express more often.

 EXERCISE 2.5: *"Try On" New Traits*

Look over the traits in the box below. Circle or list the traits that are most true for you. Put a square around it or list the traits you would like to strengthen.

Trait Box

Active, adaptable, adventurous, aggressive, aloof, altruistic, analytical, approval-seeking, artistic, assertive, athletic, attentive, bossy, calm, caring, cautious, certain, charismatic, charitable, charming, cheerful, clever, compassionate, compliant, collaborative, competent, competitive, concerned, condescending, conscientious, confident, confrontational, congenial, considerate, contemplative, courageous, creative, critical, curious, cynical, decisive, diplomatic, direct, dishonest, disorganized, dramatic, dynamic, easygoing, emotional, empathic, energetic, enthusiastic, extroverted, fair, fearful, flexible, friendly, frivolous, fun-loving, funny, generous, giving, happy, headstrong, honest, humorous, impatient, impulsive, innovative, intellectual, intense, intolerable, introverted, inventive, kind, liberal, logical, loving, loyal, mean, moody, neat, needy, negative, nervous, obedient, obsessive, open-minded, opinionated, organized, outgoing, passionate, patient, pensive, perceptive, persistent, persuasive, positive, practical, pushy, rational, relaxed, respectful, responsible, rigid, rude, sad, self-centered, selfish, sensible, sensitive, serene, serious, shy, snobbish, sociable, sophisticated, spontaneous, stable, stingy, strong, stubborn, temperamental, thoughtful, thoughtless, tidy, timid, tolerant, truthful, uncaring, understanding, unique, unselfish, upbeat, uptight, vigilant, vulnerable, warm, wild, whimsical, witty, zany

---

Identify your strongest traits:

_____   _____   _____

_____   _____   _____

_____   _____   _____

Which traits would you like to add or strengthen?

_____   _____   _____

Are there any traits you would like to minimize or change? Which ones?

_____   _____

Why?

_____

_____

_____

What could you do to improve them?

_____

_____

_____

> "All of us have the potential to embody all manner of human qualities ...we encompass all possible human dimensions and polarities although we may not be in touch with them."
>
> —Jennifer Mackewn
> Organizational Consultant, Author

Choose one trait to focus on this week. In what way(s) will you apply this trait?

EXAMPLE: *I will practice being more outgoing this week by introducing myself to new people.*

*I will practice being*_____   *by* _____

_____

_____

Identify and Manage Your Emotions

Part of self-awareness, is being able to recognize the emotions you experience on a daily basis. Noticing and identifying a specific feeling as it occurs is known as having emotional awareness. Once you are in tune with your emotions, you are best equipped to manage the response.

Identifying emotions is easier when things are going well and your desires are being met. For example, if your team wins a game, you may notice feeling happy, elated, proud, and delighted. However, it can be more challenging to name your feelings when your needs aren't being met. In these cases, people can sometimes avoid their feelings by engaging in unhealthy behavior. Notice what feelings arise when your team loses. Do you get around those feelings by saying that you didn't care anyway, walk away, get angry, or blame someone else? Or do you accept and manage your feelings in a healthy way?

Managing emotions is a matter of choice. Once you can name your emotion, such as, "I'm feeling *discouraged* right now, because my interview with a client didn't go as well as I had expected," then you're in the best position to deal with it. You could choose, a more favorable option such as taking a walk and letting some time go by before deciding on your response. This "wait" time can help you distance yourself from the state of your emotions, so as not to be reactive or hasty with your response.

> "It's through naming and acknowledging our emotions that we actually learn to manage them, rather than letting ourselves be consumed by them."
>
> —Wendy De Rosa,
> Intuitive healer and Author

In addition, recognizing your emotions can provide better communication with others. For example, when you're feeling rejected, you could say, "I felt hurt when you didn't call me back last night." Conveying your feelings to another, can often help to clarify and resolve the situation. The use of "I" statements is further discussed in chapter three, "Dare to Communicate."

Yumi shared an apartment with three other girls who were best friends. They shared common interests, which often left Yumi to feel like the odd girl out. One evening the roommates called a meeting to let Yumi know she wasn't living up to their expectations of cooking and grocery shopping. Yumi worked longer hours than the others and felt hurt and embarrassed by their accusations. All she wanted to do was run away from them. In her anger, she decided to move out. Yumi found another apartment, and was gone by the end of the week.

Yumi had let her strong emotions overrule her decisions. Perhaps this living arrangement wasn't the best situation for Yumi, however, her choice to move out was based on her emotional reaction.

 **EXERCISE 2.6:** *Make Decisions without Reacting to Strong Emotions*

In the story above, what could Yumi have done instead of moving out? What were her options? Write your ideas below.

Yumi could have:

_____

_____

_____

In the following exercise, you will examine a list of feeling words that can help you more accurately identify and communicate your emotions. This list provides only a sampling of the multitude of emotions we are able to experience.

EXERCISE 2.7: *Express Your Emotions*

1. Think about a positive situation you've had with a friend, co-worker, or romantic partner. Describe your experience:

_____

_____

_____

What feelings or emotions occurred? Use the chart below to identify your emotional state at the time.

I felt _____ *when* _____

_____

_____

2. Think about an unpleasant situation you've had with a friend, co-worker, or romantic partner. Describe your experience:

_____

_____

_____

What feelings or emotions occurred? Use the chart below to identify your emotional state at the time.

I felt _____ *when* _____

_____

_____

Feelings of satisfaction:

Happy	Confident	Peaceful	Engaged	Loving
glad	empowered	calm	interested	devoted
joyous	proud	centered	excited	ender
jubilant	secure	quiet	curious	sweet
elated	safe	content	absorbed	warm
satisfied	hardy	mellow	fascinated	caring
resourceful	strong	okay	ntrigued	gracious
eager	poised	fulfilled	stimulated	touched
energetic	certain	comfortable	alert	respectful

Feelings of dissatisfaction:

Angry	Depressed	Confused	Sad	Anxious
enraged	empty	lost	unhappy	nervous
furious	powerless	uneasy	lonely	worried
irate	sulky	unsure	downhearted	concerned
livid	ashamed	hesitant	grieved	apprehensive
resentful	down	awkward	tearful	restless
bitter	disappointed	doubtful	unworthy	jittery
spiteful	hopeless	shy	fragile	worried
critical	miserable	ambivalent	gloomy	alarmed

What Are Your Highest Priorities?

The qualities that are most important to you are called **values**. They represent your highest priorities that ultimately guide your decisions. Some people strive for wealth or achievement while others may seek living a spiritual life. The more you stay true to your values, the more self-assured and confident you will be.

Co-workers liked having Tamika on their projects because she always followed through with what she said she would do. Her team could count on her to be on time and give candid feedback. It bothered Tamika when some of her co-workers didn't complete the tasks, they said they would do. She preferred to be with people who followed through on their commitments, as she did. Tamika's actions at work showed her personal honesty and integrity. Those were qualities she valued in herself and in her colleagues.

> A fun online Values Test to take can be found at: https://www.thegoodproject.org/ (Search under Resources for Value Sort.)

Being clear on your values can help establish a sense of purpose and bolster your confidence. It can also lead you toward your vocation or career.

Brittany discovered courage and helping others as two of her core values. Because of her strong values she decided to become a paramedic and save the lives of those who require emergency help

> "Here are the values that I stand for: honesty, equality, kindness, compassion, treating people the way you want to be treated and helping those in need. To me those are traditional values."
>
> — Ellen DeGeneres, American Comedian

One way to discover your values is to select them from a list, see exercise 2.8. Another way is to look at what annoys you in others. For example, if a friend who often doesn't keep her word bothers you, then *honesty* and *integrity* may be a strong value for you. Or, you may find you dislike being around people who are too serious. In that case, having fun and enjoying life may be what you value.

In the next exercise, you will look over a list of values and see which ones stand out for you.

EXERCISE 2.8: *Determine Your Values*

From the list of values below, circle or write on a separate paper 10 values that are most important to you. These represent the guidelines for how you choose to live your life. Next, narrow your list to your top four. You may need to combine those values that seem similar.

Values List

Achievement	Community	Courage	Creativity
Environment	Faith/Spirituality	Family	Freedom
Fun/Enjoy Life	Generosity	Gratitude	Hard Work
Health/Fitness	Helping Others	Honesty, Integrity	Humor
Independence	Kindness	Leadership	Love/ Relationships
Love of Learning	Openness/Curiosity	Optimism	Perseverance
Personal Growth	Power/Influence	Professional Accomplishment	Quality/ Careful Work
Recognition/Fame	Self-Improvement	Social Justice/ Fairness	Solitude
Success	Teaching/Mentoring	Timekeeping/	Wealth/Material Well-Being

What are your top 4 values?

_____ _____ _____ _____

In what way(s) do these values show up in your life now?

- _____
- _____
- _____

In what way(s) might your values influence your future plans/career?

- _____
- _____
- _____

EXERCISE 2.9: *Your Attributes Chart*

Look back over your results from the exercises in this section. List your information in the chart that follows. When completed, you will have an at-a-glance view of your highest attributes. Notice if some of them appear in more than one column.

> "Knowing yourself is the beginning of all wisdom."
> — Aristotle, Greek Philosopher

Strengths/ Interests	Personality Characteristics	Strongest Traits	Your Values

"When you start seeing your worth, you'll find it harder to stay around people who don't."

—Unknown

"If you're presenting yourself
with confidence,
you can pull off
pretty much anything."

—Katy Perry, American Singer

DARE TO
Be Confident

KEY POINTS TO REMEMBER

1. Self-confidence is knowing who you are and taking pride in it.

2. Play on your own team. Do not be in opposition to yourself.

3. Act toward yourself with the respect you would give a good friend.

4. It is up to you to take care of your needs including physical, mental, emotional, and spiritual.

5. Take the time to learn and pursue activities that make you happy.

6. Those who honor their core strengths and interests, tend to live happier lives.

7. Trying on new traits helps expand your experiences.

8. Your values represent your highest priorities that ultimately guide important decisions.

9. Personality assessments can give insight into attributes you may have undervalued.

10. When you own and accept who you are, your confidence shows!

Dare to Be Confident
Post-Quiz

After completing the exercises in this chapter, please take a few weeks or so to practice the concepts and then retake this quiz to check your progress. Also, the quiz can be taken at a later date to reassess your needs.

Directions: Read each statement below and put a √ in the column that best reflects how well that fits for you at this point in your life.

Confidence Qualities	Not Yet	Rarely	Often	I Got This!
I treat myself as I would a best friend.				
I believe I am unique and deserving of happiness.				
I know my strengths and talents and am proud of them.				
I actively seek out things I'm most interested in.				
I am comfortable with who I am.				
I know what is important for my happiness and success.				
I use positive and encouraging language towards myself.				
I deserve all the good things that life has to offer.				
I am involved in hobbies and activities that interest me.				
I take care of my physical, mental, emotional, and spiritual needs.				
I honor my values and priorities.				
I practice self-care.				
I stand up for my needs, wants, and desires.				

How did you do? Did you experience any new discoveries? Did any of your checkmarks move into the next column? If you have any remaining √ in the *Not Yet* or *Rarely* columns, what actions might you take to what action steps might you take to move forward in that area?

Dare to Take Action

1. After completing this section, did you gain some insights or realizations about your life? What "Aha!" moments did you discover?

   - _____
   - _____
   - _____
   - _____

2. What goals or small action steps might you take to be more confident and self-assured? (It's helpful if you can be specific about what you will do and when you will do it.) Complete the following statement: *"I will take pride in who I am by..."*

   EXAMPLE: — *posting my values on my desk and staying true to them every day.*

   — *meeting people who share my interests starting on Monday.*

   — *eating at least one nourishing and healthy meal each day.*

   - _____
   - _____
   - _____
   - _____

❖ ❖ ❖

"We do not need magic to change the world, we carry all the power we need inside ourselves already..."

—J.K. Rowling, British Author

❖ ❖ ❖

3

DARE TO
Build Successful Relationships

Develop strong interpersonal communication skills.

{ "Mutual caring relationships require kindness and patience, tolerance, optimism, joy in the other's achievements, confidence in oneself, and the ability to give without undue thought of gain." }

— Mr. (Fred) Rogers, American Television Personality

How Easily Do You Connect with Others?

Two of the important abilities in life are being able to connect and communicate well with others. These abilities are often referred to as social skills. These skills are not only important in your personal life, but essential in the workplace. Most jobs today require regular interactions with co-workers, customers, and/or clients. Therefore, it is imperative to be able to communicate effectively both verbally and nonverbally.

Many of the young women I coach, struggle with meeting new people and communicating their needs to others, especially true in the workplace. They want to feel valued, but often have difficulty asking for a raise or promotion. Knowing how to effectively communicate, valuing one's own skills, and appreciating the uniqueness of others is indispensable in today's market. Most companies are looking for employees with good "people" skills in addition to their experience.

In this section, you'll learn various ways to communicate, strategies to help you better connect with others, and the art of conversation. In addition, you'll gain a better understanding of compassionate relationships and how to create healthy boundaries. At the end of the section, you'll work towards creating your own network of people who will encourage you and support your success.

The quiz on the following page can help you get started. Learn how well you connect with others now and then retake the quiz at the end of the chapter to see if your communication skills have grown.

Dare to Build Successful Relationships
Pre-Quiz

How well do you make friends and build positive relationships? Take this quiz to determine your current ability to connect with others. You'll retake the same quiz at the end of the chapter to see if your relationship skills have grown.

Directions: Read each statement below and put a √ in the column that best reflects how well that fits for you at this point in your life.

Relationship Strategies	Not Yet	Rarely	Often	I Got This!
I treat people with respect.				
Meeting new people and making conversations is easy for me.				
I know what I stand for.				
I smile when I'm around others.				
I am curious about other people.				
I do what I say I am going to do.				
I am comfortable around people who are different than me.				
I show compassion for others who suffer.				
I am comfortable making eye contact with others.				
I convey confidence through my words and my actions.				
My friends and/or associates respect my boundaries.				
I am a good listener.				
I make an effort to connect with others.				

The statements in the *Often* or *I Got This!* column are qualities you already possess. The statements marked in the *Not Yet or Rarely* columns are behaviors that you can develop and strengthen as you work through the activities. Retake the quiz at the end of the chapter to check your progress.

The Art of Conversation

Some people make friends more easily while others feel shy, often not knowing what to say. However, with a few tools and best practices, anyone can learn to make new friends and build caring relationships.

Jessica was a brilliant math student. She spent much of her time by herself working on school projects. She tended to avoid joining clubs or groups, not knowing how to approach people. For Jessica, it was much easier to work alone than to reach out to others.

> "I'm pretty good with not being afraid to just go up to people and introduce myself."
> — Elle Fanning, American Actress

Kayla, on the other hand was popular in school. She was outgoing and easily connected with others. Jessica envied her. She wanted to be more outgoing like Kayla and have friends, but froze up whenever she met someone new.

Kayla had a natural curiosity about those around her. Her focus was on them and not about how they would perceive her. Jessica, tended to dwell on her own insecurities focusing her attention more inward than outward. Rather than conversing with class-mates, she self-consciously worried about saying or doing the wrong thing. Jessica could benefit, as Kayla did by reaching out to others with curiosity and by taking a genuine interest in them.

Many people believe that trading stories equals good conversation. One-person shares their latest experience of a bad job interview, and the other person rather than learning more about the incident, chimes in with her own terrible interview experience. While this exchange of stories is common, it is not the best way to connect with others.

> "You can make more friends in two months by becoming interested in other people than you can in two years by trying to get other people interested in you."
> — Dale Carnegie, American Writer

The optimum way to carry on a conversation is to follow these four steps (4 A's) to great communication: *Attend, Acknowledge, Ask,* and *Advise.*

1. **Attend**: Listen intently to what the other person is saying. Listen for their viewpoint and how they feel about their experience.
2. **Acknowledge**: Acknowledge that you heard them by recognizing their feelings, such as, "You must have felt frustrated during that interview."

3. **Ask**: Be curious about what the person is trying to convey to you. Ask questions that deepen the understanding, such as, "What was that like for you?"

4. **Advise**: Offer your advice or your own story only after your friend has shared hers fully. Also, when giving advice it is best given as a thought or an idea, for example, "One idea might be to make an appointment with your boss," versus telling the person what to do, "You should make an appointment with your boss." Do you see the difference?

When you use these four A's, your friend or colleague will not only feel heard, the relationship can deepen. Also, remember the best tool in conversing with others is to be curious about them. Show an interest in who they are and what they are trying to convey. Focusing on the speaker will keep you from being distracted by your own sense of unease or awkwardness.

 EXERCISE 3.1: *Practice Listening*

The next time you have a conversation with someone, practice focusing on what they are saying rather than thinking of what you plan to say next. Listen intently and ask questions to keep the conversation going. If your friend was sharing a concern with you, were you able to follow the four A's or did you jump to sharing your story or advice-giving?

> "Connection is the energy that is created between people when they feel seen, heard, and valued; when they can give and receive without judgement..."
>
> — Brené Brown, American Author

Write about your experience on the lines below. How easy or difficult was it for you to keep the conversation going by listening to what the other person said? What could you do to improve upon your interactions?

_____

_____

_____

_____

_____

Types of Communication

Any time you interact with another person, you're using social skills which may include any combination of verbal, non-verbal, written, and visual communications.

Having effective communication skills is important to building rewarding relationships in your personal life and in the work environment. Deliberately, paying attention to both your choice of words along with your nonverbal language, can help you become a more confident communicator.

When verbal and nonverbal messages are aligned, they can help to make a message strong. However, if they don't match, they can cause confusion and perhaps distrust. For example, if I say I like you (verbal) and am smiling and looking directly at you (nonverbal), then both forms of communication match. If I say I like you while rolling my eyes and grinning, I'm giving mixed messages.

> **If you struggle with listening, practice by listening to audio books or podcasts. Although everyone can improve with practice, some people have stronger auditory skills than others.**

Verbal Communication

Verbal communication involves getting a message across to another person or groups of people through the use of both oral and/or written language. This can also include sign language. There are several skills to consider when trying to communicate effectively and efficiently both orally and written, such as:

- **Setting Your Tone**: Do you want to come across in friendly, funny, serious, casual, sad, sarcastic, or in a more formal manner? This can depend largely on your audience and the way in which you want to be perceived.
- **Speaking Confidently**: Plan what you want to say and speak with clarity. Avoid being vague.
- **Connecting from the Heart**: Speak from your truth by being honest and genuine.
- **Own Your Statements**: Take ownership of your words by using "I" statements. This helps the listener understand what your beliefs and feelings are, such as, "*I feel hurt when you forget to call me,*" or "*I feel better when I work out at the gym.*"
- **Avoid Collective "You" Statements**: This use of "you," distances the speaker from the thought by not owning their own words, such as, "*You always feel bad when your friend forgets to call,*" or "*You always feel better when you work out at*

the gym." The use of "you" is used in a general sense, not speaking directly to the individual.

- **Avoid "You" Statements that Blame**: The use of "you" can also put blame on the other person such as, "You rarely call me anymore." This puts the other person in a defensive position. Instead, own your truth by saying, "I often feel hurt when you don't call." This helps you take responsibility for your own needs.

Communicating in a more confident manner by using "I" statement takes practice. It helps others know exactly where you stand. Thinking about your personal and professional relationships, in what way(s) might this skill be most effective?

_____

_____

 EXERCISE 3.2: *A Letter of Appreciation*

Make a positive connection by writing a letter or email to someone you admire. This can be a teacher, relative, celebrity, co-worker, author, artist, etc. Write the letter letting them know what it is that you appreciate about them. Use "I" statements to share your thoughts and feelings. Be specific, as shown in the following example.

EXAMPLE:

Dear Ms. Martin,

I'm writing this note to let you know how much I appreciated the extra time you took in reviewing my manuscript. I very much admire your ability to attend to detail and for the clear feedback you provided. Thank you for being such a supportive friend.

Sincerely,
Connie

Dear _____ ,

_____

_____

_____

_____

Nonverbal communication

Nonverbal communication is also called body language and communicates without the use of words. Your body can convey your mood, feelings, intentions, and interests. It can show the person how well you are listening and can also express your level of confidence.

These include:

- making eye contact
- smiling
- nodding
- facial expression
- touch
- body posture
- gestures
- tone of voice
- posture

Making eye contact is an important part of good communication and can sometimes speak louder than words. Your eyes provide a connection with others which can convey your mood, feelings, intentions, and interests. They can let the other person know you are listening and paying attention to them. Eye contact can also signal a sense of confidence which is helpful in building trust and respect with a co-worker or a friend. It's best to briefly break eye contact now and then to keep the conversation casual and not so intense.

Avoiding eye contact can also convey a message to the other person, perhaps indicating you don't want to be honest or don't feel comfortable with them. This avoidance can leave the other person unclear about your intentions.

When meeting with a small group, be sure to maintain eye contact with the speaker to let them know you are paying attention. People who are working on tasks or checking their phones, signal to the speaker that what they are saying isn't important. When speaking to a small group, slowly rotate your gaze from person to person every 5-10 seconds, or so.

If you're uncomfortable making eye contact due to feeling shy, it's best to start practicing with those you are most comfortable with. Observing how others make eye contact can also be beneficial. When you look at the other person, look at the point between their eyes in a soft and gentle way. Looking now and then, can help you gain more confidence.

What body language do you think conveys confidence?

_____

_____

What body language do you imagine conveys a lack of confidence?

_____

_____

Which non-verbal behaviors will you focus on this week, such as smiling more, practicing eye contact, or improving posture?

_____

_____

I-Thou and I-It Relationships

Martin Buber, a famous philosopher, referred to relationships in two ways: I-Thou and I-It. Simply put, the I-Thou relationship is horizontal, human to human; whereas, I-It interactions tend to be vertical and hierarchical.

In I-Thou relations the "I" acknowledges the other as a multi-faceted living being deserving of respect and dignity. For example, if you encounter a complete stranger sitting on a park bench, you can enter into an I-Thou relationship by merely thinking positive thoughts about that person. You see her as a person with needs and feelings similar to your own. It is akin to the Golden Rule where you treat others with the same care and compassion as you would want to be treated. Whether it is a person, a tree, or another type of creature, the "I" recognizes the worth and value of the other and their relevance in this world.

In an I-It relationship, a person or groups of people are perceived to be more important than others, where in truth everyone has value and deserves to be treated as such. I-It relations often occur in the devaluing or diminishing of others, where a person is not seen as whole but rather by certain aspects of themselves, such as: _He's a jock, She's hot,_ or _They're nerds._ When a person is objectified in this way they are being treated as a commodity or an item without regard to their personality or dignity as a human being. Those that treat people this way lack compassion and empathy for others.

EXERCISE 3.3: *I-Thou and I-It Connections*

On the lines below, write about your relationships with others at school or in the workplace. Notice if your interactions are I-Thou or I-It in nature. How do you, for example, treat the grocery clerk, bus driver, or a new employee?

Write about a situation where you or others you know have treated someone in an I-It way. How could that encounter have been changed to a more respectful one?

I-It Situation: _____

_____

To I-Thou: _____

_____

What could you do to show your I-Thou connections with other living beings?

_____

_____

_____

Create Healthy Boundaries

Creating healthy boundaries is about setting limits about how you will allow others to treat you. This means being clear about what behaviors you find acceptable and unacceptable. It is about being in integrity with who you are and not letting others derail you.

Picture an imaginary circle that surrounds you. Let's call this circle, your *Circle of Integrity*. This circle represents the entirety of you: your strengths, gifts, talents, personality, preferences, interests, and wants and desires. When you stand strong within your circle, you are powerful, taking pride in who you are and staying true to your values. As Brené Brown says, "You know what's ok for you and what's not ok for you."

This imaginary circle represents the interpersonal boundary between yourself and others. It shows others what they can expect from you; as well as how you expect

> "Boundaries are a clear understanding of what's ok for you and what's not ok for you."
> —Brené Brown, American Author

to be treated by them. Standing confident in your circle helps you be assertive, speaking up when others mistreat you.

> *Brenda's boyfriend was inconsistent about going out with her. He would say he would call at a specific time and then fail to do so. This seemed to be happening more frequently. Brenda would stop making plans expecting and waiting for him to show up at any time. She was allowing him to pull her out of her Circle of Integrity, and she felt miserable.*
>
> *After confiding with a respected mentor, Brenda realized that her boyfriend had been treating her in a way that was disrespectful and uncaring, and she didn't deserve it. Brenda chose to talk with her boyfriend and let him know what she expected from him. She was direct and to the point saying that he either showed more respect or she wasn't interested in dating him anymore. Brenda, truly liked him and it wasn't easy for her to ask for what she needed. However, she realized, that if she didn't value herself, he nor anyone else would either.*

Being out of your circle is like a helium balloon that has been let go and is flying around without direction or guidance. When this happens, your emotions are off balance and you're unable to feel good about yourself. When you're grounded in your circle, your self-confidence shows.

 EXERCISE 3.4: *Stand in Your Circle of Integrity*

On the lines below, write about a time when you were pulled out of your *Circle of Integrity*. What happened? How did you feel? If you had a chance to do it over again, what would you do differently?

> **EXAMPLE:** *I was pulled out of my Circle of Integrity when a co-worker piled extra work on me with little regard for my already heavy work load. I did the work without saying anything to her. Looking back, I would have spoken up and let her know it wasn't okay and that she would have to find another solution.*

I was out of my Circle of Integrity when _____

_____

_____

_____

Looking back, I would act differently by _____

_____

_____

_____

_____

_____

When you choose to go along with pressure from others, you will find yourself pulled out of your Circle of Integrity. Being out of your circle can cause feelings of anxiety and self-doubt because you have not honored your inner truth. When you stay in your circle, other people, including bullies, have difficulty getting you to do things you don't want to do.

> "Be who you are and say what you feel, because those who mind don't matter and those who matter don't mind."
> — Dr. Seuss, American Author

{ "Whether it is a friendship or a
relationship, all bonds are built
on trust. Without it,
you have nothing." }

—Unknown

DARE TO
Build Successful Relationships

Key Points to Remember

- Caring relationships require kindness and joy in others' achievements without undue thought of gain for yourself.

- Listening in a deep way is important to having productive conversations.

- Practice the 4 A's for growing relationships: *Attend, Acknowledge, Ask*, and *Advise*.

- Nonverbal communication, such as eye contact, smiling, and nodding, is important when trying to connect with others.

- Use "I-statements" to take ownership of your thoughts and ideas.

- Ask open-ended questions to keep a conversation going, rather than exchanging stories.

- Show empathy by taking the perspective of others.

- I-Thou relationships treat others as equals showing respect and kindness. I-It relationships are vertical in nature by treating others as objects, rather than as people with feelings and needs like everyone else.

- Know what you stand for and how you want to be treated by others.

- Stand in your Circle of Integrity and surround yourself with people who show you respect.

- Believe in yourself and in your ability to make positive relationships!

Dare to Build Successful Relationships
Post-Quiz

After completing the exercises in this chapter, please take a few weeks or so to practice the concepts and then retake this quiz to check your progress. Also, the quiz can be taken at a later date to reassess your needs.

Directions: Read each statement below and put a √ in the column that best reflects how well that fits for you at this point in your life.

Relationship Strategies	Not Yet	Rarely	Often	I Got This!
I treat people with respect.				
Meeting new people and making conversations is easy for me.				
I know what I stand for.				
I smile when I'm around others.				
I am curious about other people.				
I do what I say I am going to do.				
I am comfortable around people who are different than me.				
I show compassion for others who suffer.				
I am comfortable making eye contact with others.				
I convey confidence through my words and my actions.				
My friends and/or associates respect my boundaries.				
I am a good listener.				
I make an effort to connect with others.				

How did you do? Did you experience any new discoveries? Did any of your checkmarks move into the next column? If you have any remaining √ in the *Not Yet* or *Rarely* columns, what action steps might you take to what action steps might you take to move forward in that area?

Dare to Take Action

1. After completing this section, did you gain some insight or realization about your relationships? What "Aha!" moments did you discover?

    - _____
    - _____
    - _____
    - _____

2. What goals or small action steps might you take to develop respectful relationships, both personally and professionally? (It's helpful if you can be specific about what you will do and when you will do it.) Complete the following statement: *"I dare to acquire strong social skills and healthy, respectful relationships by...*

    EXAMPLE: — *practicing making better eye contact with my boss this week.*

    — *meeting someone new each week day.*

    — *choosing my words carefully when speaking to my friends.*

    - _____
    - _____
    - _____

◆ ◆ ◆

"We could learn a lot from crayons; some are sharp, some are pretty, some are dull, while others bright, some have weird names, but they all have learned to live together in the same box."

– Robert Fulghum, American Author

◆ ◆ ◆

DARE TO
Be Fearless

Recognize the obstacles that keep you stuck.

{ "It's not the absence of fear,
it's overcoming it.
Sometimes you've got to
blast through and have faith."

—Emma Watson, American Actress }

What Holds You Back?

Do you ever find yourself avoiding something challenging? Perhaps you began seeking a college degree, but then decided to drop out convincing yourself it wasn't for you. Or, perhaps, you'd like to ask for a raise, become a writer, or quit a senseless job. Whenever you find yourself giving up and remaining stuck, fear is often lurking beneath the surface. Fear is a strong sensation that can keep you from getting what you want. Understanding how it works can help you push through it.

Fear can be an asset. It is an instinctive human emotion designed to keep you safe from harm and is vital to survival. For example, when you come up against a perceived threat, like entering a building smelling of gas or hearing footsteps behind you when walking the streets late at night, your body might alert you as it spontaneously reacts to the danger. You may experience a physical response such as a rapid heart rate, shortness of breath, sweating, and/or trembling. Your body is preparing for action, either to attack or run, otherwise known as the "fight or flight" response.

Unfortunately, the same fear-provoking physical sensations can appear in situations not threatening bodily harm. They can occur when you, for example, attempt something challenging, like taking an important exam or speaking in front of a large audience. These actions can invoke a fear of rejection, failure, or feelings of being out of control.

As Emma Watson states, "Being fearless is not being without fear" it is about recognizing it and moving forward anyway. Underneath all fear, according to Susan Jeffers, in her bestselling book, *Feel the Fear and Do It Anyway,* is the fear of not being able to handle life's challenges. Recognizing the difference between real danger and perceived danger is important in managing fear.

As you work through the activities on the following pages, you will gain a better understanding of the nature of fear and how it keeps you playing safe thus doubting your own abilities. Take the quiz on the next page to see how well you manage the obstacles that hold you back. Then retake the quiz at the end of the chapter to check on your progress.

Dare to Be Fearless
Pre-Quiz

How well do you deal with issues of uncertainty? Take this quiz to determine your current ability to manage your worry and self-doubt.

Directions: Read each statement below and put a √ in the column that best reflects how well that fits for you at this point in your life.

Daring Qualities	Not Yet	Rarely	Often	I Got This!
I manage my inner critical voice.				
I'm comfortable taking risks.				
I'm able to push through my fears.				
I can begin a project without procrastinating.				
I know how to manage stress and worry in healthy ways.				
I notice when I limit myself.				
I take steps toward achieving my goals.				
I don't let feelings of guilt or shame hold me back.				
I take care of my body and mind in healthy ways.				
I can handle life's ups and downs.				
I don't allow worry to get in the way of my goals.				
I use kind versus unkind self-talk.				

The statements in the *Often* or *I Got This!* column are qualities you already possess. The statements marked in the *Not Yet or Rarely* columns are behaviors that you can develop and strengthen as you work through the activities. Retake the quiz at the end of the chapter to check your progress.

The Inner Critic

Everyone, young and old, has the voice of the critic in his or her head. Sometimes this voice can sound like and mimic a person in your life: a parent, a teacher, a colleague, a minister, or a friend. The critic presents itself as a pessimistic, discouraging voice that at times compares you unfavorably to others thus shaking your confidence. This voice might say things like, *"You're overweight, "You don't know what you're doing," "You don't look good in your clothes,"* and so on. The critic constantly insults you, trying to keep you safe from the pain of rejection and failure. Its goal is to frighten you, keeping you from taking risks and making changes in your life.

Sometimes, the critic shows up in the middle of the night or when you first awaken in the morning saying things like: *"You should have gotten up earlier to exercise,"* or, *"You shouldn't get up so early; you need to get more sleep."* Your inner critic can sometimes be relentless trying to control you by making you wrong no matter what you do.

When you venture out or try something new, the inner critic reprimands you with words like, "Why can't you do anything right?", "What's wrong with you?", or "Who do you think you are to try that?" The voice tries to trigger fear when no real danger is present. It will try every trick in the book to keep you from taking risks, wanting you always to play it safe.

In the example below, notice what happens to Jamie, a high school grad, who was planning to go to college and study law. Her parents, searched for the best colleges and found one in another state, which they believed would be advantageous for her. However, Jamie's inner critic sensed this was too risky and tried to keep her from moving away. Here's what the exchange between Jamie and her critic sounded like inside her head:

Jamie: *I want to become a lawyer and there's a great college in New York.*
Inner Critic: *You'll be too far away from home. You won't be able to handle it.*
Jamie: *My parents say this is a perfect place for me, and I think it sounds good.*
Inner Critic: *You won't know anyone there. How will you be able to survive not having your friends around? You know you can't manage that. And you're really not smart enough to become a lawyer, anyway. Who are you to do something so lofty? You'll never make it. You'll fail.*
Jamie: *This feels very scary. Maybe I should wait a year and go to our nearby community college.*

Does this sound like anything you've heard playing out in your own head? Notice how Jamie's inner critic didn't back down and how it tried to keep Jamie from venturing out too far? Hence, Jamie began rationalizing reasons to back away from her initial objective. She feared being unable to handle this new venture, even though it had been her longtime goal.

The Critic's Tricks

The critic uses many tricks and disguises in an attempt to control you. It is a master at mimicking and amplifying the voices of other people in your life who have tried to diminish you in the past. The following is a list of some of the most common critics. See if any of them sound familiar to you.

- **The Shamer**: This critic likes to use words like "should" and "must" over and over in an attempt to shame and control you. The Shamer's intent is to put unrealistic and unreasonable demands on you in an attempt to keep you from having fun and experiencing life. The Shamer says things like, *"You must go to the gym four times a week,".* or *"You should be making more money."* The Shamer tells you that you "must"

> Replace *should* and *must* with *could*. The word, could is encouraging and less demeaning: "I *could* have done better on that exam," or "I *could* work harder."

or "should" be a certain way in order to protect you from being rejected by others.

Ginger, a college grad, was afraid to meet new people. When invited to a networking function put on by a women's group, The Shamer tried to keep her from attending by saying things like, "You look terrible in clothes. You should stay home and not risk embarrassing yourself."

With a critic like that, no wonder Ginger avoided meeting new people. How can Ginger dare to be fearless when her inner critic is so loud, convincing her to be afraid?

Addictive behaviors may also result from your critic's need to shame you into compliance by making you feel inadequate and imperfect. You can feel so completely diminished that you seek things that can give you instant pleasure thus avoiding the pain of the critic's harsh words. Unfortunately, these behaviors are often unhealthy and can result in further emotional pain.

Addictions are generally associated with a physical or psychological dependence on a potentially harmful substance such as alcohol, drugs, or tobacco. Addictive behaviors can also include gambling, overeating, over-exercising, gaming, and other repetitive activities.

When your actions become unmanageable and self-destructive, seeing a trained healthcare professional is essential, especially with regard to drugs and alcohol addictions, which can be life-threatening.

Tip: Listen carefully for your critic's "should" or "must" statements, making you feel guilty for not measuring up. Instead, reframe the statements with "could," *"I could work out several times this week,"* or *"I could make more time to study."* The word "could," sounds more encouraging and less demeaning. Mistakes are part of learning and don't define you as a person. The key is to learn from your disappointments and not beat yourself up over them. Turning to addictions only make things worse.

- **The Perfectionist**: This critic declares that you must do things perfectly or you will not be liked or valued by others. The critic's pressure is so strong that you begin feeling anxious and have trouble getting started. You find yourself *avoiding* and therefore, *procrastinating*, by putting off the inevitable. Your work ends up being completed at the last minute and most likely not your best. The Perfectionist gloats at being right. She reminds you that you aren't good enough and therefore it's best that you don't even try.

For example, Samantha was having a tough time in college. Sometimes she would miss classes because she just couldn't face another boring lecture. She'd put off assignments until the last minute, and then feel a sense of disdain for herself when her grades came back low. The Perfectionist admonished her for not measuring up to its highest standards and urged her to drop out of school. "You don't need college anyway," the critic urged, "just get a job and make your life simple."

In truth, Samantha, wasn't the "loser" as her critic painted her out to be. Her goal was to graduate and she was still on track to do so. Without the constant pressure and distorted judgement of The Perfectionist, Samantha might have realized she was actually doing better than the critic let her believe.

Tip: When you notice yourself putting off a task, check to see if your inner critic is pushing you to have unreasonable expectations. Notice if you worry about what others might think of your work and fear their disapproval. The best way I've found to counter The Perfectionist is to let my work be *"good enough"* instead of needing it to be *"perfect."*

- **The Judger**: This particular critic is relentless in comparing you unfavorably to others in an attempt to make you feel inferior and unworthy. The Judger, causes you to feel envious of others saying things like, "Why aren't your grades as good as Rachel's? Or, "Jessica looks so slim, why don't you look like her?"

> Envy occurs when a someone wants something another person has. Jealousy, is when you feel threatened by another person taking away something you already possess or think you possess.

The Judger might say, *"Watch out for your friend, Courtney. She's trying to steal your boyfriend."* Or, *"Why does your mom spend more time with your sister than you?"* causing you to feel jealous of others.

In both cases, your inner critic tries to shame you by comparing you harshly to others. The critic believes it is keeping you safe by keeping you feeling inferior.

Tip: Notice when you're feeling envious or jealous of someone. Attempt to catch The Judger in the act of trying to make you feel inadequate or deficient in some way. Ask yourself if The Judger is being truthful or is she exaggerating the situation in an effort to control you? Also, check out whether or not you actually want what the other person has, and if you do, decide if you are willing to put out the effort to make it happen.

- **The Liar**: This critic tries to derail you by distorting the truth, causing you to feel confused and unsure of yourself. Look at the following three examples of the critic's negative and erroneous thinking to see if you recognize these undesirable patterns in yourself:

1. Catastrophizing: When you *catastrophize,* you believe that situations are bigger than they really are and that they affect you far more than they actually do. Your critic makes you think that if you have a problem in one area of your life, it will occur in other areas, as well. For example, if you have trouble being

motivated at work, the critic has you believe you are a totally unmotivated person, when that most likely isn't true.

2. Filtering: *Filtering* is a type of negative thinking where you see only the worst elements of your life. For example, do you focus on a low score you've received instead of emphasizing the high marks? The critic has you filter out the positive and dwell on the negative, leaving you feeling miserable. Your critic wants you to believe you have zero redeeming qualities, which we rationally know can't be true.

3. Personalizing: *Personalizing*, means you believe what others say and do is about you rather than realizing it is mostly about them. For example, a good friend may seem to be ignoring you because she hasn't returned your phone calls. Rather than checking it out with her, your inner critic has you believing she's unhappy with you and that it's your fault. Perhaps her reason is not about you at all.

> **What people think, say, and do is generally about them.**

Tip: Take notice when you're feeling down, as though life is giving you lemons. Try to uncover what The Liar is saying to you, because it is always trying to hide the truth from you. Your job is to counter the critic by seeking out the facts, rather than falling for her lies.

EXERCISE 4.1: *Spot the Critic*

Did you notice any of the aforementioned critics in your life, such as *The Shamer, The Perfectionist, The Judger*, or *The Liar*? Remember, these critics cause self-defeating behaviors such as *perfectionism, procrastination, jealousy, envy, catastrophizing, filtering*, and *personalizing.*

In the space below, write about a self-defeating behavior you or someone you know might have. What fear and shame might be lying beneath this behavior? Write about those experiences below:

EXAMPLE: *I have a tendency to procrastinate clearing off my desk. Sometimes I don't know where or how to begin. I think The Shamer and The Perfectionist convince me to feel bad about being so sloppy and that I'm worthless.*

_____

_____

_____

_____

_____

_____

_____

_____

Managing Your Critic

Unfortunately, the voice of the critic is almost impossible to get rid of. But, it can be muted by first noticing it and then calling it out for what it is.

Once you hear your critic, see if you can put a name to it in order to minimize its hold on you. Perhaps your critic sounds like one or more of the ones named previously like The Judger or The Liar. Or, perhaps, your critic has a different name.

The author, Rick Carson, called the critical voice, "*Gremlin*" in his book, "*Taming the Gremlin.*" He talks about overcoming and subduing the "nasty beast." He presents a comical way to understand the hold the inner critic can have on you.

In the following exercise, call out your monster with a name and a face. What does your critic look and sound like? What is its name?

> "Your gremlin is the narrator in your head. He has influenced you since you came into this world, and he accompanies you throughout your entire existence. He's with you when you wake up in the morning and when you go to sleep at night.
>
> He tells you who and how you are, and he defines and interprets your every reality, and his goal, from moment to moment, day to day, is to squelch the natural, vibrant you within."
>
> — Rick Carson, American Author

 EXERCISE 4.2: *Draw Your Critic*

As you go about your day, listen for the voice of your inner critic who's keeping you from trying something new or challenging. What does this voice sound like? Is it male or female? Is it loud or soft? Does it sound like someone you know?

In the space below or on a separate page, draw your inner negative voice. Imagine your critic as someone who is funny looking, ridiculous, vulnerable, or outrageous. One of my clients drew Darth Vader as her judger. Another chose Cruella as her shamer.

Another option in lieu of drawing could be to find a picture that closely resembles the voice you hear. Posting your drawing or picture where you can easily see it, can remind you of the critic who's trying to sabotage you living your most daring life.

Draw/insert and name your critic below. Specifically identifying the creature makes it real and therefore easier to defuse.

Your Critic's Name: _____

Quieting the Critic

In order to quiet the critic, you must turn down its volume and turn up a more positive voice. You can create an inner mentor whom you can imagine has your best interests at heart. Or, you can use your own voice to encourage and motivate you which is referred to as positive self-talk.

- **The Inner Mentor**: Instead of only listening to your inner critic's voice, you can create a more supportive and nurturing one.

> **"You've always had the power my dear, you just had to learn it for yourself."**
> — Glinda, The Good Witch in The Wizard of Oz

This inner mentor exemplifies someone who wants the best for you. It can be the voice of someone you know, a person from history, a fictional character, or someone of your own creation. One of my clients chose as her mentor, a favorite aunt, who was a professionally successful woman.

Nancy Drew, the famous fictional detective, has always been my inner guide. She inspired and motivated me for decades to live my life with adventure and courage. I keep her picture and books in my office as a reminder to be a more confident risk-taker.

Imagining your own nurturing mentor is a great way to ignore the critic and listen to a wiser and more encouraging voice.

 EXERCISE 4.3: *Your Nurturing Mentor*

Choose a person or fictional character to be your internal mentor. Draw a picture, make a clay model, use a photograph, a figurine, or find an illustration that best represents your guide. Be sure to keep the image where you can see it often as a reminder of the unconditional support you need and deserve.

My inner mentor is: _____

I chose this person because _____

_____

_____

_____

_____

- **Positive Self-Talk**: Positive Self-Talk is another tool you can use to help manage your fear. Positive self-talk is simply your own voice urging you to push through self-doubt. For example, if you fear asking for a raise, your positive self-talk can encourage you by saying, "You deserve this," or "Go ahead and take a chance." Positive self-talk is a powerful way to get through tough challenges just as Wanda did.

Wanda entered a triathlon race. She had been training for months and knew she was ready. Unfortunately, the first leg of the race was swimming in the lake. This was Wanda's least favorite part of the competition.

When she got in, it was so cold she couldn't put her head in the water. This was causing her to lose her timing. If this continued, she would be disqualified from the race. Her inner critic tried to get her to quit by reminding her that she wasn't a strong swimmer and she wouldn't be able to manage in the freezing conditions.

> Imagine if you believed you could handle whatever comes your way...you would be Fearless!

Wanda turned down the volume of the critic and began to use her positive self-talk. She told herself, "Just do three breast strokes and then paddle for a bit, you can do that and then see what happens." She coached herself to do five the next time and then six. Soon she was able to put her head in the water and swim ten at a time. With her self-talk, Wanda finished the swimming portion and headed to the next stage of the race. Self-talk helped her push through her fear.

EXERCISE 4.4: *Using Positive Self-Talk*

Think about some of the barriers that you have in your life right now. What issues or circumstances are in the way of you being happy and successful? Perhaps, you're struggling in one of your courses, having difficulty deciding what college to attend, or what career path to take.

On the lines below, list 3-5 problems that are preventing you from stepping forward in your life. Next to each issue, write the words of encouragement you could use to help move you through this stuck place you're in.

Issue

EXAMPLE:
Trouble making friends.

Positive Self-Talk

Example:
Make one nice comment to someone in the cafeteria. You can do this. People like you.

_____   _____

_____

_____   _____

_____

_____   _____

_____

{
"If you hear a voice within
you say, 'You cannot paint,'
then by all
means PAINT and that
voice will be silenced."

— Vincent Van Gogh, Dutch Painter
}

DARE TO
Be Fearless

KEY POINTS TO REMEMBER

- Beneath all self-doubt is the fear of not being able to handle life's challenges, including fear of failure and disappointment.

- Fear is an instinctive human emotion designed to keep you safe.

- Everyone, young and old, has the voice of a critic in her head.

- Feelings of shame are marked by words like "should" and "ought." Replacing them with "could" is a kinder approach.

- When you envy another person, you want something they have.

- Jealousy occurs when you feel threatened by another person taking away something you already possess.

- Negative thinking occurs when you filter out the positive aspects of your life.

- Imagining a nurturing mentor can provide you with support, love, and courage whenever you need it.

- Positive self-talk is a tool to motivate you through fear and self-doubt.

- Allow yourself to make mistakes. You can handle it!

Dare to Be Fearless
Post-Quiz

After completing the exercises in this chapter, please take a few weeks or so to practice the concepts and then retake this quiz to check your progress. Also, the quiz can be taken at a later date to reassess your needs.

Directions: Read each statement below and put a √ in the column that best reflects how well that fits for you at this point in your life.

Daring Qualities	Not Yet	Rarely	Often	I Got This!
I manage my inner critical voice.				
I'm comfortable taking risks.				
I'm able to push through my fears.				
I can begin a project without procrastinating.				
I know how to manage stress and worry in healthy ways.				
I notice when I limit myself.				
I take steps toward achieving my goals.				
I don't let feelings of guilt or shame hold me back.				
I take care of my body and mind in healthy ways.				
I can handle life's ups and downs.				
I don't allow worry to get in the way of my goals.				
I use kind versus unkind self-talk.				

How did you do? Did you experience any new discoveries? Did any of your checkmarks move into the next column? If you have any remaining √ in the *Not Yet* or *Rarely* columns, what action steps might you take to what action steps might you take to move forward in that area?

Dare to Take Action

1. After completing this section, did you gain some insight or realization about fear and how it keeps you stuck? What "Aha!" moments did you discover?

    - _____
    - _____
    - _____

2. What goals or small action steps might you take to go after what you want? (It's helpful if you can be specific about what you will do and when you will do it.) Complete the following statement: *"I dare to conquer the obstacles that hold me back by…*

    EXAMPLE: — *enrolling in a computer course tomorrow that I have been avoiding.*

    — *apologizing to a friend this week whose feelings I hurt.*

    — *noticing when I'm envious of others, and reframing my thoughts.*

    - _____
    - _____
    - _____

❖   ❖   ❖

*"To me, fearless is not the absence of fear.
It's not being completely unafraid. To me,
fearless is having fears. Fearless is
having doubts. Lots of them.
To me, fearless is living in spite of
those things that scare you to death."*

—Taylor Swift, American Singer

❖   ❖   ❖

DARE TO
Have It All

Design the Daring Life You Want!

{
"Maybe young women don't wonder
whether they can have it all
any longer, but in case any of you
are wondering, of course you can
have it all. What are you going to do?
Everything, is my guess."

— Nora Ephron, American Journalist
}

Dare to Have It All

I love the quote by Nora Ephron on the previous page, where she asks, "What are you going to do?" Everything, is my guess." In those two lines she challenges you to go beyond the limitations set by others and go after all you can with confidence and courage. The key is to discover what you want and know that you are deserving of it all.

As you Design Your Daring Life, you may want to look back on the things you learned from the previous chapters. In Chapter One, you explored possibilities for your life. You created a Dream It board to uncover your inner desires. In addition, you brainstormed what an ideal life might look like in the eight areas of life and began a list of all that you want to achieve during your lifetime.

Chapter Two, took you on a deep dive into your personality, interests, and talents. You gained further insight into your super powers, by taking one or more personality assessments. You learned about your strong traits and the qualities you'd further like to experience.

In Chapter Three, you acquired the necessary skills to communicate with others and how to treat people in an I-Thou manner. In addition, you identified your circle of integrity and what it means to have healthy interpersonal boundaries.

In the previous chapter, Chapter Four, you learned about fear and how it can keep you from living your best life. You discovered various critics that attempt to hold you back and how to minimize their influence over you. You also learned strategies to push through and overcome that fear.

In this final chapter, you'll take the knowledge you've acquired thus far and set your intentions for the life you want to live. In addition, you'll acquire five essential tools to help boost your positive outlook and ultimate success.

Be sure to take the quiz on the next page to check where you are in terms of your readiness to go after your goals. Then retake the quiz at the end of this chapter to reassess your progress.

Dare to Have It All
Pre-Quiz

How well do you set goals and plan for your future? Take this quiz to see where you stand.

Directions: Read each statement below and put a √ in the column that best reflects how well that fits for you at this point in your life.

Success Strategies	Not Yet	Rarely	Often	I Got This!
I am a positive person.				
I set intentions for my life.				
I create small goals to achieve my long-term goals.				
I have a positive mindset about myself and my future.				
I believe I can learn new things.				
I am flexible and adaptive.				
I know how to motivate and encourage myself.				
My work and home space are organized.				
I know what I want and am willing to make it happen.				
I am surrounded by people who are supportive of me.				
I feel motivated about my future.				
I take responsibility for my thoughts and actions.				

The statements in the *Often* or *I Got This!* column are qualities you already possess. The statements marked in the *Not Yet or Rarely* columns are behaviors that you can develop and strengthen as you work through the activities. Retake the quiz at the end of the chapter to check your progress.

Create Intentions

Choosing what you want in life and choosing what actions to take are at the very foundation of *Designing Your Daring Life*. You are in the driver's seat for choosing what you want and then creating a plan to make it happen.

> "Intentions are causes that create effects. Choosing an intention is the fundamental creative act. An intention is the reason or motivation for doing what you do."
>
> —Gary Zukav, American Spiritual Teacher, Author

Setting an intention is what guides and motivates your every decision. It is the why behind what you do, and can clarify how you want to be, live, and show up in the world. For example, an intention around work might be, *"I intend be a team-player with my co-workers."* Or, a personal intention might be, *"I intend to live a creative and beautiful life."*

Intentions are written in a way that shows how you want to be rather than what you will do. They are typically written in a brief and clear manner indicating your motive or reason for your actions. Intentions can be short-term, such as *"I intend to be more organized today."* Or they can be longer, such as *"I intend to be an expert in marine biology."*

 EXERCISE 5.1: *Create Short Term Intentions*

1. You can start Designing Your Daring Life right now, by writing out a few intentions for this week. Intentions offer a roadmap for how you choose to be and how you want to feel. For example, "I intend to be a kinder person," or *"I intend to be on time."* Intentions guide the reason for your actions.

    On the lines below, write a few intentions for this week:

> "Setting an intention is like drawing a map of where you wish to go—it becomes the driving force behind your goals and visions. Without an intention, there is no map, and you're just driving down a road with no destination in mind."
>
> — Source Unknown

I intend to be _____

_____

I intend to be _____

_____

2. Choose one intention and brainstorm what you can do to make it happen. A mind map is an excellent tool to brainstorm any ideas because it sorts items in the same way your brain does. What can I do to achieve my intention? See the mind map below.

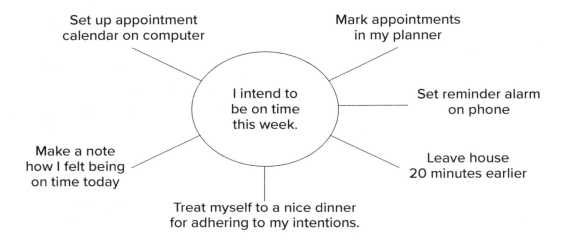

3. Draw a circle in the space below and write one intention for this week in the center as previously shown. Next, brainstorm the action-steps/goals you can do to achieve that intention. See how many ideas you can generate.

4. Which action(s) will you take this week?

Action item #1: _____

_____

Action item #2: _____

_____

> "Intentions are like magnets. The more we declare them, believe in them and act in ways to manifest them, the more powerful and real they become."
> — Source Unknown

EXERCISE 5.2: *Create Long-Term Intentions*

1. What intentions do you want for your future? How do you want to show up in the world in the areas of work, relationships, spirituality, health, physical surroundings, personal growth, finances, humanity, and so on?

For this exercise, write an intention for work and/or for your personal life. When writing your intention statement, make sure it feels true for you.

For example, a personal intention might be, *"I intend to be well read and informed."* An intention in the area of work could be, *"I intend to have a job that pays well."*

Work: I intend to be _____

Personal Life: I intend to be _____

2. On a separate piece of paper, draw a mind map for your intention(s) and then brainstorm the action-steps/goals you could take.

3. Which action-steps/goal(s) will you focus on?

_____

_____

_____

_____

_____

4. Next, fill out the lines below to create your own roadmap/plan for your Daring Life

EXAMPLE:

- *Intention: "I intend to help young women create their life goals.*
- *Goal: To become a school counselor.*
- *Action Steps:*
  - *Interview a school counselor to learn about that career*
  - *Research a degree program*
  - *Research the salary*
  - *Research the role/responsibilities of a school counselor*
  - *Investigate the requirements*
  - *Investigate college programs*
  - *Enroll in a college*

Your Roadmap:

- *Your Intention: _____*
- *Your Goal: _____*
- *Action Steps:*

  - _____
  - _____
  - _____
  - _____
  - _____
  - _____

Tools for Happiness and Success

In order to achieve success, I recommend the following five additional tools and approaches to help you live your happiest life:

Tool #1: Be "in Choice"

You are always "in choice" no matter your situation or circumstance. Every moment of every day you are choosing what you think, what you say, and ultimately what you do.

Being "in choice" means you take responsibility for your decisions and actions. This is one of the most important steps in creating the life you want because you realize it is most likely up to you. This includes not only your ultimate decision making, but your mental attitude, as well.

> "What people have the capacity to choose, they have the ability to change."
> — Madeleine Albright, Former United States Secretary of State

When you say, "I do this because I have to," according to Dr. Marshall Rosenberg, "you are actually shirking responsibility for your actions and putting the blame elsewhere. And when you blame others, it detaches you from being an active participant in your life."

Deborah and Kayla were roommates. Because Kayla worked longer hours than Deborah, Deborah took on the responsibility of cleaning their apartment. She hated spending each weekend mopping the floors and scrubbing the bathrooms, but didn't feel she had any choice because those things, she believed, had to be done. "I do this because I have to," Deborah stated over and over. She felt like a victim because she believed her circumstances kept her from going out and having fun with friends.

In reality, it was Deborah's choice to cleanup. No one was making her do it. Although she believed it was her duty, it ultimately was her decision to make. She needed to ask herself why she was choosing one stance over another.

Once Deborah understood the concept of choice, she was able to admit that she had wanted to live in a neat and spotless home environment, which was the true reason for her actions. Deborah in the end took responsibility for her motives and felt more in control of her life. She no longer saw herself as a victim. In addition, she was able to communicate to her room-

> "Above all, be the heroine of your life, not the victim."
> — Nora Ephron, American Journalist

mate, her need for a clean and tranquil environment. Do you see how we are always "in choice" for what we think, what we say, and what we do?

EXERCISE 5.3: *Take Responsibility*

In what way(s) do you blame others for your actions or inaction?

> **EXAMPLE:** *I blame my parents for rescuing me every time I fail. They're responsible for my failure.*

Write your "blames" on the lines below.

> "Everything can be taken from a man but one thing: the last of human freedoms—to choose one's attitude in any given set of circumstances, to choose one's own way."
>
> — Viktor E. Frankl, Austrian Holocaust Survivor, Psychiatrist

_____

_____

_____

_____

_____

As you Design Your Daring Life, what does the statement, "You are always in choice,"
mean to you? _____

_____

_____

_____

Tool #2: Get Organized

1. Clearing out the physical clutter in your life makes for a great intention. Imagine how you will feel when all of your belongings are neatly organized and easily accessible. When organizing your living or work environment, it's helpful to make a sketch of where you want your furniture to go and where you want to store your papers and materials. Most professional organizers recommend using the sorting plan by dividing your things into three piles or categories: 1) Keep and put away, 2) Donate, 3) Throw away. There are many channels on YouTube.com devoted to all types of organizing techniques. Each channel provides a great way to help you get started.

EXERCISE 5.4: *Getting Things in Order*

Write an intention around being more organized. What area(s) of your life need structure and management? How might things be better for you if things were better arranged and organized?

> "Getting organized is a sign of self-respect."
>
> — Gabrielle Bernstein, Motivational Speaker

EXAMPLE:

- *Intention: "I intend to live in an organized environment.*
- *Goal: To organize my office space.*
- *Action Steps:*
    - *Sort my papers.*
    - *Clean out my desk drawers.*
    - *Make a list of items I need and get rid of the rest.*
    - *Purchase a file cabinet.*
    - *Purchase colorful file folders.*
    - *Find cups to store colored pens.*
    - *Purchase a good desk lamp.*

Fill out the lines below to create your own intention

- *Your Intention:* _____

- *Your Goal:* _____

- *Action Steps:* _____

    - _____

    - _____

    - _____

    - _____

    - _____

    - _____

2. Purchase a planner/calendar or use a digital one to assign dates and times to each action item that you listed above. Some actions may take a day and others may last much longer. Use your planner to calendar each task.

> I found the *Panda Planner*, works best for me to stay motivated and organized. It incorporates positive psychology by focusing on wins, passions, wishes, goals, along with areas for projects and creative designs.

Choosing the best planner/calendar for your particular needs is important. Some planners are colorful with a unique theme while others are unadorned. Many calendars either begin each week with Sunday or Monday. While this is a personal choice, it can be an important one as you create the habit of recording all of your activities in this one place.

You'll want to include appointments, projects, goals, and other important information in your planner. Finding the system that works best for you is key to being successful and achieving your goals. You may need to try a variety of methods before you find the one that works best for you on a consistent basis.

Tool #3: Choose Your Mindset

Choosing your mental attitude is an integral part in achieving success. Carol Dweck, professor at Stanford University, developed the concept of a *Fixed Mindset* (Closed) versus *Growth Mindset* (Open).

People with a fixed way of thinking believe that the factors in life are permanent. They believe that this is how life is and there is nothing that can change it. They tend to be inflexible, defensive, and often feel defeated.

Conversely, those with a growth mindset believe people can evolve and grow. They look for opportunities to expand their situation. They tend to believe that,

- Intelligence can be improved.
- Mistakes are appropriate because we learn from them.
- Giving up is not an option.

> "In a growth mindset, challenges are exciting rather than threatening. So rather than thinking, 'Oh, I'm going to reveal my weaknesses,' you say, "Wow, here's a chance to grow.'"
>
> — Carol S. Dweck, American Psychologist

- Staying open and curious allows for new ideas to develop.
- Seeking self-improvement expands for growth and opportunity.
- Life is rarely permanent. Everything is always changing.

When you are willing to explore your options and expand your knowledge, you are on the road to creating a happy and fulfilling life.

 EXERCISE 5.5: *Adopting A Learner's Mindset*

As Carol Dweck said, "For twenty years, my research has shown that the view you adopt for yourself profoundly affects the way you lead your life. It can determine whether you become the person you want to be and whether you accomplish the things you value."

Answer the questions below to examine and improve your mindset.

1. Can you think of a time when you had a limiting belief about yourself? Perhaps you believed you couldn't be a good speaker or paint beautiful pictures. In what way(s) have you limited yourself with a closed mind?

_____

_____

_____

What could you have done to change your Fixed Mindset to a more open one?

_____

_____

_____

2. Is there something you want to achieve right now that could use a Learner's Mindset? What could you do to make it happen?

_____

_____

_____

3. Listen for "yeah, buts." Those are excuses you give yourself when faced with a challenge. Such as, "Yeah, I want to get my degree, but I'm just not cut out for it." What "Yeah, buts," are you telling yourself?

_____

_____

_____

Tool #4: Make Use of Affirmations

Affirmations are positive statements designed to encourage and motivate you to achieve your goals. They are similar to "positive self-talk" as discussed in Chapter 4, but more deliberate and intentional. They are usually written out ahead of time rather than in the moment.

> "Once you replace negative thoughts with positive ones, you'll start having positive results."
>
> -Willie Nelson, American Musician, Activist

When creating an affirmation, it is important to choose words that support and acknowledge your highest vision such as, "I allow myself to be who I am without judgment."

A few guidelines for writing affirmations include:

1. Use "I" to keep your statements personal to you.
2. Keep them short and to the point.
3. Choose positive declarations; avoid negative statements such as, "Don't do ..."
4. Write it as a fact, as if you're doing it already, such as, *"I am a graduate."*
5. Avoid statements that don't align with what you believe or want for yourself.

 EXERCISE 5.6: *Write Your Affirmations*

On the lines below, write out a few affirmation statements that can best support you in achieving your intentions and goals, such as:

"I make the right choices for my life."
"I treat myself with kindness."
"I maintain a positive attitude while working on my project."

"I love who I am and who I am becoming."
"I am fulfilling my passion and purpose in life."

_____

_____

_____

_____

Tool #5: Build a Support Team

In order to be successful and achieve your highest dreams, be sure to surround yourself with people who are in harmony with those things that are important to you. Look for people, clubs, or organization that are aligned with your values (Revisit Chapter Two). For example, if education is a strong value, you may want to join a teacher's organization, where like-minded people would surround you.

Everyone needs to be with caring and encouraging people who can challenge and support him or her when things get tough.

> "Find a group of people who challenge and inspire you, spend a lot of time with them, and it will change your life forever."
>
> — Amy Poehler,
> American Actress

 EXERCISE 5.7: *Build Your Team*

Draw a circle in the area below or on a separate piece of paper.

Write the names of the people, groups, or organizations in the circle that encourage and support you to be your best self. These can be people who have given you confidence in the past, those who currently cheer you on, or those you would like to be on your team. Next, be on the lookout for people or groups to add into your circle.

{ "Make a conscious effort to surround yourself with positive, nourishing, and uplifting people—people who believe in you, encourage you to go after your dreams, and applaud your victories." }

— Jack Canfield, American Author

DARE TO
Have It All

Key Points to Remember

- A person with a fixed mindset believes that who they are is permanent. They don't believe their life can be improved or changed.

- A person with a growth mindset is curious about life, believing that change can occur. They believe giving up is not an option.

- When you are flexible, active, and curious, you are open to possibilities for yourself and for others.

- You are always at choice. No matter your circumstances, what you think, say, and do is up to you.

- Creating an intention means you decide how you want to show up in the world. It explains who and how you want to be. It is the incentive behind your actions.

- Your intentions are often based on your values, talents, or interests. They can also be built from your purpose for being on this Earth.

- Goals are action-steps based on intentions.

- "If you want to live a happy life, tie it to a goal, not to people or things." — Albert Einstein

- Live your life on purpose!

Dare to Have it All
Post-Quiz

After completing the exercises in this chapter, please take a few weeks or so to practice the concepts and then retake this quiz to check your progress. Also, the quiz can be taken at a later date to reassess your needs.

Directions: Read each statement below and put a √ in the column that best reflects how well that fits for you at this point in your life.

Success Strategies	Not Yet	Rarely	Often	I Got This!
I am a positive person.				
I set intentions for my life.				
I create small goals to achieve my long-term goals.				
I have a positive mindset about myself and my future.				
I believe I can learn new things.				
I am flexible and adaptive.				
I know how to motivate and encourage myself.				
My work and home space are organized.				
I know what I want and am willing to make it happen.				
I am surrounded by people who are supportive of me.				
I feel motivated about my future.				
I take responsibility for my thoughts and actions.				

How did you do? Did you experience any new discoveries? Did any of your checkmarks move into the next column? If you have any remaining √ in the *Not Yet* or *Rarely* columns, what action steps might you take to what action steps might you take to move forward in that area?

Dare to Take Action

1. After completing this section, did you gain some insight or realization about your life? What "Aha!" moments did you discover?

    - _____
    - _____
    - _____
    - _____
    - _____

2. What goals or small action steps might you take to go after what you want? (It's helpful if you can be specific about what you will do and when you will do it.)

    In order to design the daring life I want,

    — *I will set short and long-term intentions.*

    — *I will research careers that interest me.*

    — *I will take responsibility for my words, actions, and thoughts.*

    - _____
    - _____
    - _____
    - _____

    - To be 100% encouraging and supportive of myself!

◆　◆　◆

"What you do makes a difference, and you have to decide what kind of difference you want to make."

—Jane Goodall, English Primatologist and Anthropologist

◆　◆　◆

Final Words

After completing the activities and concepts in this book, I hope you're well on your way to planning and achieving the daring life you want. As you journey forward, know that you are capable and deserving of all that life has to offer. This final activity is designed to strengthen and reinforce your belief in yourself and give you the courage to ascend beyond any lingering doubts.

In the 1941 Disney animated movie, *Dumbo*, the little elephant with big ears wanted to fly. He didn't believe he could do it, until he was given a "magic feather." With the feather held firmly in his trunk, he suddenly believed he could fly. The feather gave him the confidence and support he needed to overcome his self-doubt. With this feather, Dumbo was fearless. He didn't just fly, he soared!

Just like Dumbo's feathers, you too, can use objects, known as "anchors" to give you the confidence and courage to soar beyond your wildest dreams.

> "You're on your own. And you know what you know. And you are the one who'll decide where to go."
>
> —Dr. Seuss, American Author

 EXERCISE: *Find Your Anchor*

Find any object such as a piece of jewelry, a key, photo, coin, or some other keepsake that can be used as an "anchor" like Dumbo's "magical feather." On my desk I keep a golden Disney key as my anchor, to remind me of my own inner magic and child-like spirit. What will you choose for your anchor and how will it inspire you?

My anchor is _____ *to remind me* _____

_____

❖ ❖ ❖

"Nothing is impossible;
the word itself says 'I'm possible'!"
—Audrey Hepburn, American Actress

❖ ❖ ❖

Made in the USA
Las Vegas, NV
04 September 2021